"Garrett pointed out that I haven't been fair to you, and he's right."

"I'm not sure what you mean." Not quite true. But Nell wanted more than vague generalizations.

"I've told you I wouldn't date because of my obligations to Claire. Tonight I... sent a different signal."

"Yes."

Zeke cleared his throat and gripped the wheel tighter. "I apologize."

"For what?"

"Dancing with you so often."

"I can't speak for you, but I had fun."

"So did I. That's the problem."

"Why?"

"I think you know why."

Uh-uh. You're not dodging that question, buddy. "I'm not sure I do." A quick glance confirmed his jaw was clenched.

Silence. Then finally, as if forcing them out, he said the words. "Because I want you."

SINGLE-DAD COWBOY

THE BUCKSKIN BROTHERHOOD

Vicki Lewis Thompson

Ocean Dance Press

SINGLE-DAD COWBOY
© 2021 Vicki Lewis Thompson

ISBN: 978-1-63803-989-1

Ocean Dance Press LLC
PO Box 69901
Oro Valley, AZ 85737

This is a work of fiction. Any resemblance to actual persons, living or dead, business establishments, events, or locales is entirely coincidental.

Visit the author's website at
VickiLewisThompson.com

Want more cowboys? Check out these other titles by
Vicki Lewis Thompson

The Buckskin Brotherhood
Sweet-Talking Cowboy
Big-Hearted Cowboy
Baby-Daddy Cowboy
True-Blue Cowboy
Strong-Willed Cowboy
Secret-Santa Cowboy
Stand-Up Cowboy
Single-Dad Cowboy

The McGavin Brothers
A Cowboy's Strength
A Cowboy's Honor
A Cowboy's Return
A Cowboy's Heart
A Cowboy's Courage
A Cowboy's Christmas
A Cowboy's Kiss
A Cowboy's Luck
A Cowboy's Charm
A Cowboy's Challenge
A Cowboy's Baby
A Cowboy's Holiday
A Cowboy's Choice
A Cowboy's Worth
A Cowboy's Destiny
A Cowboy's Secret
A Cowboy's Homecoming

_1_

On this cool May evening, the logs crackling in the fire pit gave off enough heat to make jackets optional. Zeke Lassiter shrugged out of his and draped it over the arm of his Adirondack chair. Claire did the same. His daughter copied his every move these days, and setting a good example was at the top of his list.

Her face glowed in the flickering light, her blue eyes sparkling with anticipation. The Brotherhood had gathered, all except Leo, who was visiting Fiona's parents this week. Claire relished a fire pit evening more than a night at the movies. And she loved movies.

She'd scoffed at the idea of a child-sized Adirondack. She didn't care that her feet didn't reach the ground. If these chairs were good enough for the Brotherhood—aka her beloved uncles— they were good enough for her.

"Daddy, can my class stay for dinner tomorrow? We could light up the fire pit and—"

"Sorry, sweetie." Zeke hated denying her anything, but a daytime field trip with a bunch of eight-year-olds was disruptive enough. "We can't—"

"What a cool idea." Nick gestured toward the flames with his cider bottle. "They could all make s'mores for dessert."

"Ever been on a field trip, Nicholas?" Rafe eyed him over the rim of his cider bottle.

"Can't say I have. Have you?"

"One time, to a candle factory. I was about Claire's age. What a circus. The teacher lost control and some kids got into all the things they weren't supposed to."

CJ stopped strumming his guitar. "But not you, right?"

"Are you kidding? Wax is fun to play with. And chew on."

"Miss O'Connor won't lose control, Uncle Rafe. If a kid acts up, she'll have a talk with them. She doesn't stand for any nonsense."

Zeke chuckled. "I'll vouch for that."

"She bring the hammer down on you, little brother?" Jake glanced his way, a gleam in his eye.

"Not me. I'm on my best behavior when I'm in her classroom."

"Are you, now?" Jake gave him a smirk.

"Absolutely. And FYI, she's been warned to keep an eye on you."

"Fair enough." Jake laughed. "I'll be a good boy."

"Glad to hear it." After living at the Buckskin for three months, Zeke took Jake's teasing in stride and gave as good as he got. Jake didn't tease unless he liked someone, and thank God, he'd come to like his half-brother.

They'd had a rocky start, though. Jake hadn't known he existed. On top of that, Zeke looked exactly like a younger version of their two-timing father. Fortunately, Jake had forgiven him the uncanny resemblance, and a shared dislike of dear old dad had created a bond that grew stronger every day.

"I talked with the principal when we set up this field trip," Matt said. "Harland thinks the world of Miss O'Connor. He might tag along tomorrow if everything's quiet at the school."

Claire's eyes widened. "You call Mr. Kuhn by his first name?"

He smiled. "I do now because we're friends. I called him Mr. Kuhn when I was in Apple Grove Elementary. To his face, anyway. I called him other things behind his back. I was rotten."

"I don't believe you."

"Ask him. I'm sure he remembers. I made an impression for all the wrong reasons."

"But you're so nice, Uncle Matt!"

"Because Henri and Charley turned me around. If they hadn't taken me on, I'd have wound up in juvie."

"Juvie?"

"The juvenile detention center in Great Falls."

"Wow. I'm giving Gramma Henri a big hug next time I see her."

"She'll appreciate that." Matt surveyed the men sitting in the semi-circle. "This is our first shot at a school field trip. If it goes well, Henri would like to make it a regular part of our program. I want this one to go like clockwork."

"How many kids?" Garrett unscrewed the top of his cider bottle. "I missed that—"

"Twenty-three." Claire bounced in her chair.

"Plus Nell and two parents," Zeke said. "Steve's mom and Jocelyn's mom."

"*Three* parents." Claire pointed at him.

"Oh, right."

Jake sent another teasing glance his way. "It's *Nell*, is it?"

"She asked me to call her that."

"I see." Jake pursed his lips.

"Don't read anything into it. We spent a lot of time on the greenhouse for the class project. Calling each other *Miss O'Conner* and *Mr. Lassiter* sounded stupid after hours of bolting two-by-sixes."

"Sounds like sweaty work." CJ plucked the strings of his guitar and hummed *Let Me Call You Sweetheart.*

Rafe grinned. "Nothing like shared physical labor to start things off."

"Listen, there's nothing—"

"We're getting off track." Matt tilted his head in Claire's direction in a subtle signal.

Zeke could have told him Claire was a master at reading subtle signals.

Sure enough, she spoke right up. "Don't worry about talking in front of me, Uncle Matt. I've been thinking the same thing about Miss O'Connor and Daddy. They make each other laugh. But he said he's not interested."

Zeke winced as everyone's attention swung to him. Leave it to his daughter. She was an open book, which he loved about her, but....

"Not interested?" Garrett glanced at him, eyebrows raised. "You talk about her all the time."

"Because of the greenhouse." That was his excuse and he was sticking to it. "Neither one of us knew anything about growing veggies, and we wanted it to be a success story for the kids."

"And it *is.*" Claire bounced some more, making the chair squeak. "We've got lettuce and carrots and tomatoes and zucchini. *So* much zucchini."

"And Garrett's zucchini bread is the best ever," Nick said. "I ate a whole—"

"We *know*, Nicholas." Rafe rolled his eyes. Then he turned back to Zeke. "You and Nell have gardening in common and you make each other laugh. Claire likes her. What's stopping you?"

Fear. But he wasn't admitting that with his daughter sitting there absorbing every word. "It's not the right time. We just moved here and I'm still learning the ropes."

Rafe gave him a *that's BS* look.

"Besides, it's inappropriate. She's Claire's teacher. I don't think—"

"I wouldn't care, Daddy. You look so happy when she's around. You like her. I know you do."

"Well, sure. She's a nice person." What a colorless way to describe Nell, the most natural, vibrant woman he'd ever met. Her enthusiasm for life drew him like a moth to a flame. But he'd been burned before and wore the scars to prove it.

He glanced at Matt, a port in a storm. "We're getting close to Claire's bedtime. We should probably finish the planning while she's here to give us info on the kids. I know most of them, but she's the expert on the best way to divide them into groups."

Claire dug in her jeans pocket. "Miss O'Connor and I made a chart for you, Uncle Matt. To save time." She pulled out a folded piece of paper. "Since there's seven of you and twenty-three kids, you each get three, except two of you will need to take four."

Matt coughed into his fist, clearly covering his laughter. "Great. Thanks."

Wiggling toward the front of the chair until she could jump down, she marched over and handed Matt her chart. Then she came around to the side so she could explain it. "Me and my friends are the first group of four. We're high energy, so Daddy and Miss O'Connor will be in charge of us."

Nicely played. His daughter, the matchmaker.

"Uncle Rafe can also take four because Steve's mom will be in that group. Also, he's so big those kids wouldn't dare step out of line."

Nick snorted. "Unless they figure out he's a pushover."

"Am not."

"Are so, big guy."

Matt studied the paper. "You and Miss O'Connor have done a great job, Claire. Thanks."

"It was fun. We gave Uncle CJ the musical kids, plus Jocelyn's mom because she's a fan of Uncle CJ's music. Uncle Nick gets the big eaters, Uncle Garrett will take the ones who like to fix stuff, Uncle Jake needs to have the funny ones, and you get the shy kids."

"I'll consider that a compliment."

"It is. Daddy says you have a way of putting everyone at ease, which is why you're a good leader."

Matt glanced at him. "Thanks, bro."

"Just stating the obvious." He stood. "Now that we have our assignments, it's time for our field marshal to get some shuteye."

She gave him a pleading look. "But we haven't decided how the groups will rotate. Miss O'Connor suggested splitting the class in half, one for the ranch and one for Raptors Rise, and then switching places. But she said it's up to us."

"You've done the heavy lifting, sweetie," Matt said. "We can work out the rest on our own. You need your sleep. Big day tomorrow."

"Matt's right," Rafe said. "You don't want to be dragging in the morning."

"I *never* drag in the morning. I'm up like a shot."

Garrett reached out and gave her arm a squeeze. "I seem to remember you promising your dad and me that you wouldn't beg to stay up on fire pit nights. That was part of the deal."

She let out a dramatic sigh. "I should have known you'd remember that." Turning back to Matt, she pointed at the chart. "My three best friends are in my group. I'd *really* like to show them the bunkhouse first, before anyone else sees it."

"I think that can be arranged." Matt glanced up. "After all, it's your home."

She beamed at him. "Thanks, Uncle Matt. Now I can go to bed and not worry about it." She made the rounds, giving everyone a goodnight hug.

Zeke walked her back to the bunkhouse. "Kind of obvious, isn't it? Putting Miss O'Connor and me on the same team?"

"Why not? You said you like her."

"I do, but you're not going to convince me to date her."

"Because she's my teacher?"

"That, and because I'm not planning to date anyone for a while."

"But you go dancing at the Moose."

"Not the same thing."

"Have you met anyone you like there?"

"Sweetheart, I'm not looking. I just enjoy dancing and hanging out with the gang."

"Piper's parents got a divorce the same month as you and Mommy, and they're both dating. One watches Piper and her brother when the other one goes out."

"Sounds very civilized."

"You wouldn't have to worry about getting someone to watch me if you asked Miss O'Connor out. I have an open invitation at Gramma Henri's."

He groaned. "Could we please drop this subject?"

"Just let me say one more thing."

"Go ahead."

"It wouldn't be weird to ask her out on a date because she's my teacher. My friends don't think so, either."

"You've talked to them about it?"

"Of course. I talk to them about everything."

"Everything?"

"If you're wondering if I told them about Mom, yes, I did." She took his hand. "She's my mom, so I love her, but she wasn't nice to you. Miss O'Connor's nice, Daddy. And now I'll drop the subject."

Zeke's chest tightened. His daughter yearned to fill the empty space left by her uncaring mother. When the judge had granted him sole custody, he'd silently vowed to give her anything she needed. He hadn't counted on her needing this.

2

Taking her principal's advice, Nell asked the parent chaperones to be the first ones on the bus and claim seats in the back. They could supervise from the rear. Then she staked out the two front seats by laying a reserved sign on each one.

"Hey, Suzanne." She smiled at the driver.

"Big day, huh?"

"My first field trip."

"It'll be good. The kids like you. I hear them talking among themselves. They think you're cool."

"They do?" What sweetie-pies.

"Yes, ma'am."

"That's nice to know." She stepped down and joined Harland by the bus door. She'd lucked out starting her teaching career with Harland Kuhn, a seasoned educator with thirty years of experience and an endless supply of compassion.

Her third-grade class waited quietly in a reasonably straight line, exactly as they'd practiced since the beginning of the year. Today they'd lined up by shirt color, with red in front.

Her throat tightened at the expectation shining in their eager expressions. She'd fallen in love with these kids, and in another week they wouldn't be hers anymore. They'd head off for summer break and in September they'd be Valerie Jenson's fourth graders.

She cleared her throat. "Thank you for being so courteous while you waited. When you board, sit wherever you like but no more than three per seat. Once you've chosen, stay in that seat. If you need me, raise your hand and I'll come to you. I'll be in the front behind the driver and Principal Kuhn will be across the aisle from me." She stepped aside and motioned them up the steps.

Harland took the other side of the door, bestowing smiles and salutes as the kids filed past. Of average height and build, he wasn't particularly imposing until he spoke. His rich voice could calm a sobbing child or silence an auditorium filled with noisy students. She adored him and so did the kids.

Although the class had been reasonably quiet in line, negotiating their seating arrangement was a noisy affair. They chattered like a flock of sparrows at a bird feeder.

Suzanne surveyed the process with a practiced eye. After ten years behind the wheel of a school bus, she was a steadying influence. As the din subsided, she leaned toward the open bus door. "They're pretty much settled, folks."

"Thanks, Suzanne." Nell climbed in, picked up the cardboard sign and slid into her seat. Harland positioned himself across the aisle and gave her a thumbs-up before he turned to face the rows of eight-year-olds.

He was a savvy veteran of many such outings. He liked to joke that field trips were responsible for his gray hair. She, on the other hand, was a first-timer, at least as a teacher in charge. She had great memories of her own field trips at this age, though.

She swiveled in her seat and took a quick head count. Claire and Piper had commandeered the seat behind her. Riley and Tatum were in the next seat back.

The girls were inseparable. Claire's passion for horses and ranch life had drawn them together three months ago. Now all four were obsessed with having a horse of their own.

Riley had been the first to achieve it. Her parents had given her a ten-year-old bay gelding for her birthday last month. Piper's and Tatum's families lived on property that lacked the zoning for large animals, but both sets of parents had agreed to book some riding lessons this summer.

Claire was holding out for a buckskin, which meant she'd have to wait until her dad could afford one. For the bus ride, she and Piper had twisted on the bench seat so they could continue an animated debate with Riley and Tatum about the best breeds for barrel racing.

Nell had been horse-crazy at eight, too. She and her parents had lived in a high-rise in San Francisco, but that hadn't stopped her from dreaming of galloping across a flower-strewn mountain valley on a black stallion. Wasn't to be.

Not then, anyway. But now she lived in the sort of valley she'd dreamed of and she had connections to people with horses. She'd been too busy settling into her first year of teaching to take riding lessons, but summer break was right around the corner. Maybe she'd offer to take Piper and Tatum to their lessons and sign up for some herself.

"I can't wait to run the barrels this summer," Claire announced. "I get to start the first week after school's out. I'm going to practice and practice. I want to be the youngest member of the Babes."

"You need to be really good," Riley said. "I saw them perform at the Founders' Day Celebration and they go so fast, they're like a blur."

"I'm getting better at riding. Daddy and Auntie Ed—the lady I told you about who's a barrel racing champion—they say I'll be ready to start training once school's out."

The mention of Claire's father sent a tingle up Nell's spine. She'd managed to play it cool with the guy, but damn, he was one appealing cowboy. Valerie, the fourth-grade teacher who had become a good friend, had labeled Zeke too gorgeous for words.

Nell appreciated that about him. But his attitude toward his daughter had impressed her even more than his looks.

Clearly he loved Claire beyond reason. Anyone could see that. As a single dad, he easily could have spoiled her rotten. Instead he'd taught her respect, empathy and a work ethic that would put many adults to shame. She'd been a dedicated assistant during the greenhouse project.

When Nell had asked Zeke to help with that, she'd justified the impulse as an opportunity to acquaint herself with a new student and the student's parent. Yeah, right. Valerie had teased her about making that call.

But it wasn't like a romance had blossomed. Or even much of a friendship. Darn it. Now that she no longer needed him for the greenhouse project, she rarely saw him.

She'd poured out her heart to Val one night over a bottle of wine. Maybe the attraction was all on her end and she was wrong about the mutual chemistry. But no, she wasn't wrong. She had evidence.

He'd insisted on driving her home after their work sessions even though she lived within walking distance of school. When he'd handed her into his truck, he'd had that warm look in his eyes, as if he'd enjoyed the excuse to touch her.

Maybe he was uncomfortable with the concept of dating his daughter's teacher. If so, his daughter hadn't gotten the memo. She'd asked her dad to pick her up from school several times so he could see how well the veggies were growing.

Each time she'd manufactured some reason why Nell needed to accompany them to the greenhouse. And since the school day was over, he'd offer her a ride home. Eventually Nell had figured out Claire was trying her hand at matchmaking.

The field trip hadn't looked like part of her scheme until she'd mentioned that all seven wranglers, including her dad, would serve as guides. During the process of organizing the class into seven groups, she'd insisted that Nell needed to pair up with Zeke to supervise Claire and her three overly enthusiastic friends.

As Claire's teacher, she had veto power. She could have reduced the combined energy level of those girls by splitting them up. She didn't have the heart. Their friendship had the potential to last through high school, maybe even beyond. Shared memories of this field trip would be part of their history.

As for pairing with Zeke, she had no objection and Val had urged her to accept Claire's machinations and enjoy herself.

She planned to. Spending two hours with him wouldn't be a hardship. Maybe she'd figure out whether she'd misread those signs of interest on his part. And if he was hesitant because she was Claire's teacher, that barrier would be gone in—

Claire jiggled her arm where it rested along the back of the seat. "Miss O'Connor! We're here!"

Oops. She'd missed the drive in. Missed the rest of the conversation between Claire and her friends. What else had she missed? Evidently the kids had been model students. Surely she would have seen a hand waving frantically or heard the commotion if an argument had broken out.

But if the topic of Zeke had the power to distract her that much, she'd better watch herself this afternoon. She had a job to do.

"My, my, my," Suzanne murmured as she pulled the bus into the bunkhouse parking area nose first. Leaning on the steering wheel, she stared out the windshield. "If that ain't a sight for sore eyes."

Nell turned to see what Suzanne was talking about and her breath caught. Seven tall, muscular cowboys stood shoulder-to-shoulder in front of the bunkhouse, arms crossed loosely over their broad chests. "I guess that's our welcoming committee."

Suzanne kept her voice low. "They can welcome me any ol' time."

"Uh-huh." The men presented an arresting visual, especially the one wearing the black yoked shirt with silver piping and pearl buttons. One glance and her heart beat in triple time. She took a few calming breaths as Suzanne switched off the engine and opened the door.

At first she hadn't recognized him. During their work sessions, he'd dressed in a faded plaid shirt, wear-softened jeans and a battered straw cowboy hat. He'd insisted it had character. Clearly that outfit hadn't come up to the standards of today's dress code.

The yoked style of his shirt made his sturdy shoulders look even broader. The row of pearl snaps drew her attention to his impressive chest and directed her gaze down to slim hips encased lovingly in dark denim. The battered straw hat had been replaced with a midnight-black Stetson he'd pulled low over his eyes. She was totally unprepared for this version of Zeke Lassiter.

"I see your daddy!" Piper bounced in her seat.

"Me, too!" Tatum leaned forward. "Who're the other ones?"

"That's the Buckskin Brotherhood." Claire said it as if announcing a rock band about to take the stage. "My uncles."

3

Zeke was short of breath. Stupid. Today was no different from the times he'd spent with Nell putting the greenhouse together.

Except it was different, because back then he hadn't figured out the dynamic. He'd kept his admiration under wraps and enjoyed the temporary nature of their interaction. Since it wasn't going anywhere, he'd been able to relax.

Meanwhile, Claire had been building a fantasy of making them a threesome. The second time she'd suggested a visit to the greenhouse, he'd caught on. Had Nell?

He'd called his daughter on her matchmaking efforts, especially after she'd instigated this field trip. She'd insisted the outing was about sharing the ranch and the sanctuary with her class, especially her three buddies. If that meant he'd get some time with Miss O'Conner—bonus.

Judging from her comments, she was convinced she was doing him a favor. Evidently he'd hidden his emotions well. The double whammy of a cheating wife and a lying father had hit him hard, festering wounds he wasn't sure would ever heal. He still didn't know if his mom was in on the cover-up, protecting his worthless excuse for a father.

Claire didn't have the whole picture and that's how he wanted it. She might suspect that her mother had stepped out on him, but she was completely ignorant of the depth of her grandfather's deceit.

Her matchmaking was born of her innocence and optimism. She'd held onto both, thank goodness, but she'd presented him with a challenge.

School was out next week, though. If he could just get through a couple of hours today, he'd be home free. Claire would have an entire summer of barrel racing practice with Ed to distract her from this misguided strategy.

Then Nell stepped off the bus looking prettier than ever, and he doubted his ability to make it gracefully through the next two hours. A rush of pleasure heated his skin. The effort to control his reaction created tension he wouldn't be able to release by sawing two-by-sixes and drilling bolt holes.

She had on a dress today, one with little flowers on it and a skirt that swirled around her knees when she walked. He'd only seen her in a dress twice, both times when he'd caved to his daughter's request to come and admire the greenhouse. Nell had worn jeans during their work sessions, the stretchy kind that cupped her sweet little... *don't think about that, idiot!*

Her dress had a scooped neck and a filmy, spring look. She'd added a white cardigan over it.

Bet it was soft. He shoved his hands in his pockets. The urge to touch her had grown with every hour they'd spent on the greenhouse project, but his hands had been otherwise occupied with construction chores. Today, not so much.

She'd piled her dark, curly hair on top of her head in her usual way. Strands escaped from that arrangement all the time because she was constantly in motion. One afternoon he'd reached to tuck a strand back into place. And jerked his hand back before she'd noticed.

Matt walked to meet her, the chart in his hand. Nell pulled hers out of her roomy shoulder bag. After they conferred, Nell climbed back into the bus. Moments later, she emerged, followed by the students who'd take the barn tour first, including his daughter and her friends. One of the parents brought up the rear.

Jake, Nick, CJ and Rafe boarded the bus for the trip over to Raptors Rise, leaving Matt, Garrett and Zeke to lead the barn and bunkhouse tours. Nell moved with brisk efficiency, making introductions and dividing the kids into their respective groups.

As she headed toward him with four girls who were almost skipping in their eagerness, Matt and Garrett ushered their six kids over to the path that would take them to the barn.

Heart thumping, he met Nell's smile with one of his own. "Miss O'Connor."

"Mr. Lassiter."

He was glad to see her. Too damn glad. He broke eye contact and focused on the girls.

"Welcome, ladies. Ready to see Claire's living quarters?"

Their excited chorus of *yes, please* sent the doves that had been roosting in a nearby oak fluttering away.

"Easy does it, girls." Nell's hazel eyes sparkled. "You're scaring the wildlife."

"Oh!" Tatum, a tiny, delicate child with straight black hair, glanced up into the tree. "Sorry, birdies."

Claire walked closer to him and lowered her voice. "We need to start the tour with the bathroom, Daddy. I'll take them in if you want to wait out here."

"Fine with me." He looked to Nell for confirmation.

She nodded. "Sounds like a plan. Let us know when you're done."

The girls raced toward the front door.

Nell's command brought them up short. "Walk, please!"

They slowed their steps. Claire held the door for them as they walked in, their excited exclamations spilling out into the parking area as they caught their first glimpse of the interior. Then Claire stepped inside and shut the door, muting their chatter.

Nell chuckled. "I'm doubting that bathroom story."

"Me, too."

"I'll bet Claire wanted to show them the place on her own."

"Probably." And leave him alone with Nell. "She asked Matt if her girlfriends could see the bunkhouse before anyone else. He decided that was fair."

"Absolutely. This is her home."

"That's what Matt said." First time he'd talked to Nell without Claire around. Stirred him up, but in a good way. "Did your principal come?"

"He did. He stayed on the bus with the group going over to Raptors Rise."

"He was Matt's principal."

"Harland told me that when we discussed the field trip idea. Evidently Matt was a handful."

"He admits it, too." Nice to discover they could carry on a conversation without Claire to jumpstart the action. "How've you been?"

"Good." She cocked her head and gazed at him. "You?"

"Fine, thanks."

"Nice outfit."

Warmth crept up his neck. "Matt requested that we clean up a bit. He wants this field trip to go well."

"Suzanne definitely approved of your welcome party."

"Suzanne?"

"Our bus driver. Suzanne Dempsey."

"Oh, Mrs. Dempsey. I noticed she was driving today. What do you mean, she *approved*?"

"She was mesmerized by the lineup. Said it was a sight for sore eyes."

"Hm." The heat rose to his face.

"She made a good point." Laughter sparkled in her eyes. "You're a manly-looking bunch, standing shoulder-to-broad-shoulder."

"I think you like making me blush."

"I do." She grinned. "That's what you get for looking so handsome in your black shirt and snazzy black hat."

"Come on, Nell. Cut it out." Her amusement was infectious and her flirting lured him into a mood he couldn't afford. Before he could dial it back, he shot a compliment her way. "You're one to talk. That's a very pretty dress."

"Thank you. Today I felt like spring was in the air and that calls for a dress like this."

"Indeed it does." *Back away, Zeke, old boy. You know where this leads. You made a promise to yourself. Keep it.*

"Then I'm not sure why you chose to wear black. That's hardly a spring color. It's more of a… hang on." Something drew her attention toward the bunkhouse. She quickly looked away again, her color high. "Those little devils are peeking out the window." Laughter rippled through her words. "I wonder if they think we—"

"No telling." He put some distance between them and tugged on the brim of his hat.

"It's probably better if we don't overreact."

"I'm not overreacting. I just—" He sighed and shook his head.

"Is something wrong?" Her smile disappeared and a tiny crease settled between her eyebrows.

"Claire's trying to set us up."

She sucked in a breath. "I know."

"I don't want her to get the wrong impression."

"Such as?"

"That I'm going along with her plan. It's not a good idea."

"Because I'm her teacher?"

"That's part of it." He held her gaze. "The main issue is me. Claire doesn't understand. And I don't want her to. The fact is, I'm in no shape to begin a relationship."

"Because of your ex?"

"That and… other things. Claire means well and she's convinced that you and I… but it wouldn't work."

"Are you sure?"

"If we're talking about this moment in time, I'm absolutely sure." He broke eye contact and rubbed the back of his neck where a knot of tension grew. "Don't get me wrong." He focused on her again and the truth slipped right out. "I think you're wonderful. And you don't need to be saddled with a man who has enough baggage to fill a horse trailer."

"So you're warning me off."

"Yes, ma'am."

"Well, you know yourself way better than I do. But Claire's determined to bring us together and she's a very goal-oriented kid."

"Tell me about it."

Her expression gentled. "We should probably table this. If those girls' noses are plastered to the window, they're not exploring the bunkhouse. Let's go in. Maybe we'll have a chance to continue the discussion later."

"Maybe." He took a deep breath and gestured toward the bunkhouse. "Ever seen one of these?"

"Only in Westerns."

"It's something like what they show in the movies. Although I've never seen a Western where one of the bunks is filled with teddy bears."

4

I think you're wonderful. Words that inspired dreams that Nell had no business having. Zeke had flat-out told her he was a bad bet. He wasn't in favor of Claire's matchmaking.

That was a shame, because his warm humor as he conducted the bunkhouse tour lured her right in. The intimate glimpse of his modest but cozy living quarters increased her appreciation for the guy. Clearly he was determined to create a healthy, trauma-free life for his daughter.

By the time he led them through the kitchen and out the back door to inspect the fire pit, she wanted to challenge his claim that he was a bad relationship bet. Judging from his excellent parenting, he was selling himself short.

He turned the narration over to his daughter when they arrived at the stone fire pit with its semi-circle of Adirondack chairs. When he stepped back and gave her the floor, Nell walked over to stand beside him. Claire gave a vivid description of fire pit doings and her friends listened with rapt attention before peppering her with questions.

Nell moved closer to Zeke. "She loves it here," she murmured. "This setup is perfect for her."

He nodded. "Every day I thank my lucky stars that my dad told me about this place."

"Oh? How did he know about it?"

"He…um…he travels a lot." He offered the information as if it hurt his tongue.

When he didn't elaborate, she let the subject drop. Claire's grandfather must be one of the large suitcases in the baggage Zeke had mentioned.

His phone pinged and he pulled it out of his pocket. After scanning the message, he walked over toward the girls, phone in hand.

Claire glanced in his direction. "Time's up?"

"Yes, ma'am. Uncle Matt and Uncle Garrett are wrapping up the barn tour. We need to head over there."

"Woo-hoo!" Claire threw her hands in the air. "Now I get to show you the horses! Can I lead the way, Daddy?"

"Check with Miss O'Connor."

"Miss O'Connor, is that okay? I know this path like the back of my hand."

Nell smiled. "Then go for it. But no running."

"Yes, ma'am." Claire turned to her buddies. "If you think the bunkhouse and the fire pit are awesome, wait'll you see the barn. It's *incredible.* Come on." She started down a wide dirt path through the trees that was clearly well-traveled.

As usual, the girls walked in pairs. Piper, the only one who wore glasses, fell in beside Claire. Delicate little Tatum had her work cut out for her keeping up with Riley, a tall redhead, but she never complained.

Technically they didn't run. Instead they danced, twirled and skipped while maintaining a non-stop gabfest about what they'd seen and what they were about to see.

Nell glanced at Zeke as they followed behind the exuberant girls. "How far is it?"

"About a ten-minute walk."

"Then let's hold back a bit. This might be our only chance to finish our discussion."

His expression tightened. "Okay."

"Unless you'd rather not talk about it."

"No, no. It'll be good to clear the air so there are no misunderstandings."

She'd take a wild guess that he wasn't big on misunderstandings. "I get why you don't want to discuss the intimate details of your situation with Claire. But if you can't give her any reason that makes sense to her—"

"I'm counting on summer break and barrel racing practice to get her off this subject. I'll take her swimming in Crooked Creek. Garrett says fire pit nights come around more often as it gets warmer. She'll be busy."

"Sounds exciting for her."

"I'm hoping it'll work. She tends to latch onto things and not let go."

"I've observed that." She took a deep breath and plunged in. "Is Claire so wrong about us? I like you and you evidently like me. I enjoyed our time building the greenhouse."

"Me, too, but it was always going to be a one-time deal."

"You knew that before we started the project?"

"Yes, ma'am. Had to be that way. Getting sole custody was a game changer. Claire's the most important person in my life and I'll never do anything to jeopardize our life together."

That stung a little. "I would never knowingly hurt either of you."

His voice softened. "I believe that. But Claire and I are still finding our feet. The divorce is barely a year old. Coming to the Buckskin appears to have been the right move. But adding a relationship... it's too risky."

"Well, if you think so, your opinion is the one that counts."

"I'm sorry, Nell."

"Me, too. But even if we don't start dating, I think Claire will want to stay in touch with me. If she does, I want to stay in touch with her."

"I won't stand in the way of that. And maybe she will keep after me to ask you out. I'll deal with it when and if it happens. I—"

"Hey, Dad! I hear the other kids coming from the barn!"

"Me, too, sweetheart!" He looked over at Nell and lowered his voice. "She's never called me *Dad.* It's always been *Daddy.*"

"She's growing up."

"And I want that. She's an amazing young girl and she'll be even more amazing the older she gets." He swallowed. "But…"

"Part of you wants to stop time."

"Exactly. But how do you know that? You don't have kids."

"Yes, I do. I have twenty-three of them in my classroom five days a week. They've become a big part of my life. In a matter of days, they'll move on. I miss them already, and they're not even gone."

He was quiet for a moment. "I never thought of teaching like that. You spend almost as much time with Claire as I do."

"And it's nearly over." The clearing was ahead and the approaching group was in sight. She was almost out of time. "So you'll be okay with me seeing Claire after school's out, assuming she wants that?"

"Of course. You can do stuff together. I don't have to be a part of it."

"But if she can figure out a way to make you a part of it, I'll bet she will."

He sighed. "Probably. The thing is, when it comes to me, she thinks she knows best."

And maybe she does. "Then you two will have to work that out, won't you?"

"Yes, ma'am."

"Would you let me know how it goes? You have my cell number, right?"

"I do."

"No need to call. You can send me a text."

"Okay."

She breathed in a combination of fresh air and a faint scent of aftershave. Time to take a step back and let the chips fall where they may. She wasn't fond of being in that position, but it sure beat leaving the table entirely.

5

The arrival of Matt and Garrett on the path with their charges ended Zeke's private discussion with Nell, which was fine with him. He had nothing more to say.

Yes, it was a sticky situation. A complicated one, too. Claire's adoration for her teacher could make for a challenging summer requiring fancy footwork on his part. If so, he'd manage. Somehow he'd avoid an entanglement with Nell without confusing the heck out of his daughter.

Claire was certainly having a red-letter day right now. Clearly the kids who'd toured the barn had loved petting the buckskin foal, a rare treat for even the ones who had some experience with horses.

Obviously feeding carrots to Lucky Ducky had been a hit, too. Everyone was ready to trade places with Claire, live in a bunkhouse, feed Lucky carrots and visit that cute foal every day.

This was a child's paradise, a perfect place for Claire to grow and blossom. Had she figured out what would happen to her setup if he went along with her plan? What if he and Nell fell in love and wanted to create a life together?

The endgame would entail moving out of the bunkhouse Claire loved so much. If she hadn't followed her idea to its obvious conclusion, maybe it was time she did.

Matt's phone pinged with a message. "We need to move out, gang. Jake says they're winding up the Raptors Rise tour."

The adults brought order to the milling group of third-graders and Claire led her three friends toward the hip-roofed barn flanked by corrals and a large fenced pasture.

The girls hurried toward the open barn doors, but Nell paused to snap a few pictures.

Zeke waited for her. "Like it?"

"I love it." She turned to him, her eyes bright. "This is the kind of barn you see in the movies, the one I always imagined when I pretended I lived on a ranch." She tucked her phone in her oversized purse and headed for the entrance.

"You wanted to live on a ranch?"

"Oh, yeah. San Francisco never felt like home." She quickened her pace. "I always intended to teach in a small town in either Montana or Wyoming. Turned out Apple Grove had an opening and Harland fast-tracked the certification process."

"All those hours building the greenhouse and I never thought to ask how you ended up here."

"We were focused on the project."

"I suppose."

"If it weren't for Claire, I wouldn't know how you ended up here, either."

"Out of curiosity, what did she say?"

"That you recently found out about her Uncle Jake and decided to come and meet him and his new wife."

"That's the bare bones of it. I wanted to make the connection." A connection with a family member who hadn't been lying to him all his life. Someone he might be able to trust. So far, Jake had come through on that score.

The sound of giggling drifted through the door as they approached the barn. When they stepped from the sunlight to the shadowy interior, the girls were clustered around Lucky Ducky's stall. That old guy was soaking up the attention, his eyelids at half-mast as the girls rubbed his nose and scratched his neck.

Claire turned in his direction. "Did you bring carrots, Dad?"

Dad again. "Matt left a supply in a cooler in the tack room. Each group gets one bag of small chunks. We don't want to make him sick."

"That's for sure. Come on, Piper. Let's go get our bag."

"So this is the horse I've heard so much about." Nell joined Riley and Tatum at the stall door.

"You should talk to him, Miss O'Connor." Riley stepped aside to give her room. "He'll talk back to you."

"A talking horse?" Nell moved closer and stroked his neck.

Zeke had seen his share of greenhorns and she didn't act like one. She might be a city girl, but her lack of hesitation told him she'd been around horses.

"Are you a conversationalist, Lucky Ducky?" She combed her fingers through his mane. "What do you think of my class? Have you enjoyed meeting them?"

Right on cue, Lucky bobbed his head and made his signature *huh-huh-huh* sound.

"Oh, my goodness! You *do* talk."

The gelding gave an indignant snort, which made the girls laugh.

"Did I insult you?" She put a hand gently on his muzzle. "I'm so sorry." Leaning in, she gave him a soft kiss on his nose.

She'd been around horses, all right, and she loved them. One more arrow pierced his armor.

"Isn't he the sweetest horse ever?" Claire arrived and passed out the carrot chunks, one to each of the girls and one to Nell.

"He's adorable." She took her chunk of carrot and stepped back. "You girls go ahead."

"They can go first." Claire came to stand beside Nell. "I get to do this all the time. He's my starter horse. Right, Dad?" She glanced over her shoulder at him.

"He's everybody's starter horse. I'd trust him with anyone. He's a true gentleman."

"Hey, Dad, I just thought of something. Piper and Tatum want to take riding lessons." She turned to them. "Have your folks found you a place yet?"

Both girls shook their heads.

"Great! Could they come to the Buckskin, Dad? You could teach them on Lucky."

"Yeah!" Tatum bounced on her toes. "That would be so cool, Mr. Lassiter."

"It would be *awesome*." Piper twirled around and managed to catch her glasses before they went flying. "We could carpool and we'd get to see Claire and Lucky Ducky and maybe some of the other—"

"I want to come, too," Riley said.

"But you have a horse at home." Tatum stopped bouncing and faced her. "You have to learn on that one."

Her chin jutted out. "I could learn on Lucky Ducky, too."

"I don't think your parents will pay for you to learn on a different horse." Claire was in mediating mode. "But you could come along and watch."

Zeke rubbed his chin. This could work out. Another distraction to take Claire's mind off matchmaking.

"Hang on, girls." Nell glanced at him. "Mr. Lassiter hasn't said he could give you lessons. He might not have time."

Four eager little faces gazed up at him with hope in their eyes.

"I could make the time."

"Yay!!" Piper started dancing and almost lost her glasses again.

"But I'd be using Buckskin resources so I'd have to clear it with Mrs. Fox."

Claire turned to her buddies. "Mrs. Fox is my Gramma Henri."

The way she said it made him smile. Clearly she couldn't resist mentioning she had friends in high places.

"I just know she'll say yes, Daddy. You could give her a share of the money, but she'd love to have these guys come out to the ranch for lessons. She's crazy about kids."

"I'll definitely ask her." Did she revert to *Daddy* when she was asking a favor to soften him up? He wouldn't put it past her.

"She'll go for it." Claire glanced at Nell. "You probably know how to ride already."

"Actually, I don't."

Uh-oh. Hadn't seen that coming.

"You don't?" Claire looked genuinely puzzled. "You act like you do."

"I love horses. Whenever I happen to be around them, I'm always looking for a chance to pet them. But I could never spare the time or the money to take riding lessons."

"Then you should take lessons with us!"

Oh, Lordy. Claire had glimpsed an opportunity and snapped it up like the smart little cookie she was. He was both proud and dismayed by her lightning-quick response. He'd have to stay on his toes from now on.

Her three friends jumped on the idea. They figured out Nell could be the chauffeur instead of their parents, a perfect solution since she'd be coming to ride, too.

Adding an adult student probably meant adding another horse. Taking time to switch a youth saddle for an adult size would be awkward.

As the trap closed around him, she sent him a quick glance of apology. He gave her a smile in return. It wasn't her fault.

Henri probably would green-light the plan, including whatever resources he needed. Claire had Henri's number — she was crazy about kids. He and Nell would be spending a lot of time together this summer. But at least they'd have plenty of chaperones.

<u>6</u>

The Saturday after school let out, the Apple Grove Elementary faculty celebrated with their traditional bash at the Choosy Moose. Ben Malone, who owned the place, provided free food and an open bar to show his appreciation to the town's educators. Next weekend the high school faculty would get their special night.

Nell was eager to go. Even though she'd lived in Apple Grove since the start of school, she hadn't made it to the town's most famous establishment, not even for lunch. She'd had the sniffles when the group had held their Christmas party there in December.

She carpooled with Harland, his wife Alice and Valerie. As they all piled out of Harland's car, she got her first good look at her principal's outfit—yoked shirt, jeans, boots and a Stetson. "Nice duds, Harland."

"This is my Choosy Moose get-up. Alice insists on it when we go out dancing."

"You're looking sassy, too, girlfriend." Valerie smiled as she joined Nell on the sidewalk.

"I followed your advice — a skirt that swirls when I dance and a top that will get me some partners." She looped her small purse over her shoulder. "You clean up pretty good, yourself." For teaching, Valerie usually pulled her strawberry-blond hair back with a clip, but tonight she'd left it down. Her top and skirt fit the guidelines she'd given Nell.

"Thanks. I don't have your assets, but I've learned to make the most of what I have."

Alice glanced over her shoulder as she and Harland headed toward the Moose at the far end of the block. "You girls. I wouldn't be your age again for anything in the world."

"Evidently you played your cards right when you were our age," Val said. "You snagged a great guy."

"I was lucky."

"Me, too." Harland gave Alice a fond glance.

Nell lowered her voice. "They're so cute."

"No kidding. Hey, I keep forgetting to ask. Have you set up the riding lessons yet?"

"Monday and Thursday afternoons at three, starting next week. That's when Zeke has time off." Talking about it gave her the shivers. She hadn't seen him since the field trip.

"It'll be such a bonding experience for you and those girls." Val said it with a grin. She got a kick out of Claire's matchmaking efforts.

Nell swallowed a laugh. "I'm sure it will."

"Seriously, I'm a little jealous of the opportunity. I'll have the girls in September and something like this would give me a head start in getting to know them. Do you think Zeke would be willing to add me to the group?"

"I don't know. I've never done this, but with limited time..."

"Another student would mean less individual attention for everyone. I know how that goes. Never mind."

"Would you like to learn?" She couldn't tell if the lessons were a draw or if Val wanted to observe the dynamic when Claire was in matchmaking mode.

"I'd love to learn, but—"

"Then I'll ask. It might work out. Riley's just going to watch and Claire won't be taking lessons. She'll likely be her dad's assistant. And her Gramma Henri is letting us use Prince along with that older horse I told you about."

"Henri Fox is loaning out her barrel racer? Now I'm *really* jealous. That horse is primo."

"You've seen the Babes perform?"

"Every chance I get. They're poetry in motion. I love teaching, but if I could wave a magic wand and turn into a championship barrel racer, I'd be sorely tempted to switch careers."

"Really?"

"It ain't gonna happen. I'm not athletically gifted, which is one reason I've put off riding lessons. I'm afraid I'll be lousy at it, which would hurt my soul. I picture myself racing bareback across a grassy meadow."

"You, too?" Nell stared at her. "That was my childhood fantasy."

"I was all about horses when I was a kid. When I landed this job in Apple Grove, I promised myself I'd start riding lessons on my first summer break. I chickened out, convinced the reality wouldn't live up to my childhood dreams."

"It probably won't, but wouldn't it be great if it did?"

"Yeah, it would. Okay, please ask Zeke next chance you get. I don't want to rob the girls of their time on a horse, but—"

"I'll ask if it'll stretch the resources too thin. Maybe he could bring another horse into the program. They have a bunch of them out there."

Val chuckled. "That's called a herd, sweetie."

"Yeah, yeah, I need lessons in how to talk cowboy."

"But you can dance country, right?" As they neared the entrance, a lively version of a Rascal Flatts song spilled out the open door.

"I know the basics. I could probably use lessons in that, too. Do you come here a lot?"

"I used to when the person you replaced was here. She liked it. But this year I just went to the Christmas party. It's more fun with a buddy."

"I'd go with you."

"You would? You said you weren't into the bar scene."

"I can tell from the way people talk about the Moose that it isn't anything like what I was used to in San Francisco, where you just stand around drinking and scoping out who's there. If Harland, Alice and you like it, I will, too. I could brush up on my country dancing."

"And meet cute cowboys."

"Sure, why not?" Although she was stuck on a certain one. Dancing might be fun but she wouldn't be looking to meet cowboys. None of them would measure up to Zeke Lassiter.

Would he be here tonight? Probably not, if he didn't intend to date. On the other hand, she wasn't trolling for a date, either, and she was here. Clearly the emphasis was on having fun and eating good food, not hooking up with someone.

Stepping into the Choosy Moose made her sigh with pleasure. The aroma of tasty food and a spirited rendition of Tim McGraw's *Something Like That* lifted her heart. The large plush moose head mounted over the antique bar was a hoot. He sported a dark green Apple Grove High graduation cap with its gold tassel dangling on the left. A CONGRATULATIONS, GRADUATES banner in green and gold hung above him.

Dancers spun around the floor in a kaleidoscope of color as a low hum of cheerful conversation slid under the chords of the music. Yeah, she could have a good time here.

One of the cowboys on the floor executed a tricky maneuver with his partner and they grinned at each other, obviously enjoying the moment. She blinked, looked again. Zeke.

_7_

When the music ended, Zeke walked his partner back to her table. What was her name again? She'd told him when she'd asked him to dance, and he'd spaced it.

"That was fun." She remained standing as the other two women left their chairs. "I have to go. We're due at a graduation party, but I'm glad I trusted my instincts and asked you to dance before we left."

"I had fun, too." He stepped back. "Don't let me make you late for your party."

She glanced at her two friends. "Go ahead, guys. I'll be there in two minutes." As they nodded and left, she pulled her phone from her purse. "I'd like to trade digits."

He flashed her a smile. "Sorry. I dance but I don't date."

"Oh! Are you—"

"Unavailable. Much obliged for the dance, ma'am." Tipping his hat, he started back toward the gang's usual booth. He'd taken two steps when a woman sitting at a table on the other side of the room looked his way. Nell? Yep. She gave him a little wave.

Geez, now what? He should at least go over and say hello before returning to the gang. Nell's principal was part of a group that had pushed three tables together. One of the ladies looked familiar, too. She'd poked her head in a few times to say hi while he and Nell worked on the greenhouse.

Okay, he got the picture. Apple Grove Elementary had let out for the summer yesterday. The faculty was likely here to celebrate the end of the school year.

These were folks from Claire's school. Her future teachers would be in that gathering. He should absolutely say hello.

As he crossed the room Nell's expression brightened. She was glad to see him. Heaven help him, he was glad to see her, too. Couldn't help returning her smile.

Her hair was different, a mass of dark curls tumbling around her shoulders. Her blouse was cut lower than any she'd worn in his presence before. He kept his gaze on her face.

She stood. "I didn't know you'd be here."

"The gang was going and Claire wanted to have a sleepover at Henri's."

"It was her idea?"

The other shoe dropped. "Did she know about this celebration?"

"Probably. It's not a secret. The faculty's been doing this for years. The Moose's owner foots the bill. I think he and Henri—"

"Are close." Claire wasn't the only one who knew about this shindig. If it was a long-standing tradition Ben created, the entire town would know. And somehow he'd been kept out of the loop. Hmm.

"Let me introduce you to everyone."

"Thanks. That would be great." As she went around the long table, he despaired of keeping track of the names, but he zeroed in on the familiar-looking blonde lady. Valerie Jenson taught fourth grade and would have Claire next year. She acted pleased about that.

Several others commented on his daughter, too. She'd made a name for herself, which didn't surprise him. She'd also set him up tonight, aided and abetted by the Brotherhood. He should have clued in when she'd made a point of telling him to have fun.

When Nell finished the introductions, he glanced around the table. "Claire loves her school and I thank you all for giving her such a warm welcome. It's a pleasure to meet you. Now I'll let you get back to your celebration." He looked at Nell and touched two fingers to the brim of his hat. "See you Monday."

"See you then."

He left it at that and walked back to the booth where the gang sat, delighted smiles on their traitorous faces. He let out a breath. "You knew all about this, didn't you?"

Matt didn't even have the decency to look guilty. "We might've."

"Come on, Zeke." Garrett gave him a knowing look. "Don't tell us you're not happy to see her."

"That's not the point."

"Just doing you a favor, little brother."

Jake had taken to calling him that, and he didn't mind. He mostly liked it, but not tonight.

"Yeah, well, if you thought something would happen because we're at the Moose together, I hate to disappoint you. Nothing will happen."

Jake grinned. "You can say that, but Nell is headed this way even as we speak."

His heart rate picked up. His *see you Monday* comment was supposed to signal they should go their separate ways this evening. For some reason, she was bypassing that. As the Brotherhood stood to welcome her, he turned.

Nell gave them a smile. "Oh, please, sit." She waved at them, which had no effect. They continued to stand. "Okay, then. I just need to borrow Zeke for a minute, but first I wanted to find out if you got the thank-you notes from the kids."

"We did," Matt said. "Very cute. Claire's pasted them all over the walls of the bunkhouse."

"And I grabbed some to put up in the Raptors Rise visitor center," Jake said.

"That's awesome. Anyway, like I said, I just need a quick chat with Zeke." She glanced at him. "Is there a quiet corner where we can talk?"

"Um... I've never—"

"Go around the far side of the bandstand, little brother, past the end of the bar. Like you're going toward Ben's office." Jake kept his expression bland.

Didn't fool Zeke for a second. The minute they were out of sight, the speculations would begin. "Okay, thanks." He put a hand at the small of Nell's back, which seemed to be the gentlemanly thing to do since he was guiding her over there.

"I—" Nell paused to clear her throat. "I need to ask something before Monday. This seemed like the perfect opportunity."

"What is it?" Maybe they could get it out of the way before they made it to this secluded corner that had temptation written all over it.

"It has to do with the riding lesson. I was wondering if—"

The band launched full blast into Luke Bryan's *What Makes You Country*, drowning out the rest of her sentence.

He leaned down, inhaling her springtime perfume. "Never mind. We need to move upwind of those speakers."

"What?"

"Never mind!" He hustled her around the bandstand and toward the office and storage areas at the back of the building. With the speakers pointed in the other direction, they should be able to hear each other. He stopped and turned to face her. "What's up?"

She raised her voice. "I was talking to Valerie about the lessons and—"

"Hang on." He stepped closer. "There. Now you don't have to shout."

"Thanks." Her cheeks turned a pale shade of pink.

Maybe he shouldn't have moved in like that. He was close enough to feel her body heat, which made breathing normally a challenge. Backing up would be lame, so he held his ground.

She swallowed. "So Valerie would love to join our class. She'll have those girls next year and she's eager to get to know them better."

Her eyes were beautiful. He'd never been this close, never had the luxury of gazing into them when she was inches away and he could pick out the flecks of green and gold. Mesmerizing.

"So is it okay if she joins us?"

"Sure." He'd agree to just about anything if it would bring this glow of happiness to her amazing eyes.

"Thank you, Zeke. That will mean a lot to her. And me."

A couple of seconds elapsed before he figured out it was his turn to say something. "Happy to help. I may be able to use more horses for the lessons, but I'll have to talk to Henri about it. If for some reason I can't, adding another adult will mean less riding time for you."

"That's fine. I'll watch and listen. That's valuable, too."

"Yes, ma'am." He'd agreed to her request. Discussion over. Any second now she'd head back to her table. He didn't want that. Not yet, anyway. "You and Val will need hats. The girls, too."

"I figured we would."

"Boots would be helpful, the kind with a heel, but if some of you don't have them, that's okay."

"I'll pass that on."

"And sunscreen." His attention drifted to her cleavage. Such soft, creamy skin... He wrenched his attention away. "So you don't get burned."

"Good advice." She pressed her lips together, as if holding back a smile, maybe even a laugh.

"Is something funny?"

"Yes." Her smile bloomed.

"What?"

"Your effort to avoid looking at my chest."

He took a quick step back. "No, I'm—"

"Don't bother denying it."

His cheeks heated. "It's just that I've never seen you in something that low-cut."

"Valerie told me to wear a skirt that swirled for dancing and a top that would get me some partners."

That reasoning stuck in his craw. But he'd taken himself out of the game, so why shouldn't she look around for someone else? "Should work." He hesitated. "Want to dance?"

Her face lit up. "I do."

"We're probably playing right into Claire's hands."

"It's just dancing."

"You're right. Okay, let's go. That number's a slow two-step. It's a good place to start." He took her hand and led her to the dance floor. He'd never held her hand before. He liked it more than he should.

8

Nell told herself it was just a dance, no big deal. But the minute he drew her into his arms, she gave up that lie. She wanted way more than a dance with him.

She'd fought a visceral urge to claim him for a dance ever since she'd glimpsed him out on the floor with someone else.

She didn't discount the power of cleavage, either. He'd struggled against his normal male tendency to ogle. She gave him points for that.

But if the low-cut blouse had helped inspire him to dance with her, she'd take the advantage and run with it. Or dance with it.

John Pardi's *Head Over Boots* combined nicely with Zeke's mellow two-step. He was taking it easy on her and she didn't stumble once. When he flashed a smile at her as they made their way around the floor, she returned it.

His palm warmed the middle of her back, the pressure firm, confident. His dark gaze locked with hers. *Zing.* Oh, yeah, they had chemistry. She hadn't been wrong about that.

Her skirt swirled around her bare knees and her hips swayed in time to the music. *Just dancing.* Yeah, right. They were talking to each other in the subtle language of lovers. Every note, every word of the tender song wove a spell, surrounding them in a private bubble.

The song ended long before she was ready for the dance to be over.

He stopped dancing but didn't let go. "Thank you."

"I loved it."

"So did I. I'm glad you suggested it." She wouldn't mind another dance, but she was here to party with her fellow teachers and dinner should be arriving any minute. She glanced up at Zeke. "I'd like to do this again, but my meal's probably waiting. I should—"

"I'll walk you back." He slipped a hand around her waist.

And didn't she enjoy the heck out of that? Evidently she wasn't the only one affected by the dance. She savored the possessive gesture.

"I have no right to ask," he murmured, "but I'd like to dance with you again, and now that you've been out there, I guarantee other guys will—"

"What if I say I've promised all my dances to you?"

"You'd do that?" He started to smile, but it turned into a frown. "This is probably not how you intended your evening to go, but—"

"My evening is going fine. I was worried that I'd be rusty, but dancing with you is a terrific confidence booster. I want to try it again and see what happens if you throw in some complicated moves."

"Alrighty, then. I'll give you a chance to eat before I show up at your table."

"Don't wait too long. To tell the truth, I'd rather dance than eat."

"Good. Me, too."

When they reached her seat at the table, he helped her into her chair. Then he straightened and met Val's curious gaze. "Hey, Valerie."

"Hey there, Zeke."

"Nell said you'd like to take lessons with the girls."

"Only if it won't be a problem."

"Not at all. Glad to have you."

"Wow, that's great! Thanks."

He turned back to Nell. "See you soon."

"Looking forward to it."

"Ladies." He tipped his hat and headed off to rejoin the Buckskin gang.

Valerie leaned in close. "What's going on, girlfriend?"

Nell gave her a quick rundown.

Val kept her voice low. "Just dancing, huh? I'm not buying it. I saw the way he looked at you while you were out there. He's into you."

"Even if you're right, he doesn't want to do anything about it."

"Think you can change his mind?"

* * *

Would tonight's unexpected encounter make Zeke consider a relationship with her? The jury was still out, but Nell gave herself excellent odds of becoming his current favorite dance partner. He certainly was hers.

They stayed out on the floor as the band picked up the pace with several fast numbers in a row. When Zeke threw in some tricky steps, she kept up with him. Did his sexy hip movements make her fantasize how much fun they could have in her bedroom? Hey, she was only human.

When the band announced The Electric Slide, everyone in the Buckskin gang got in on it. Jake made sure Zeke and Nell were tucked into their part of the formation.

Then he took the spot next to Nell. "You haven't met my—" The music blasted, cutting him off as the group moved in unison.

"I'm Millie!" the redhead beside him called out as she pivoted. "Jake's wife!"

"Nice to meet you!"

"And that's Kate!" Jake pointed to a blonde dancing next to Rafe.

Kate waved in acknowledgment.

"Hey, this works." Jake proceeded to turn the Electric Slide into a meet-and-greet, gesturing to each of the women Nell hadn't met and calling out a name. Then he tested her, pointing at each of them and lifting his eyebrows.

She was giggling by the end of the dance.

Jake gave her a thumbs-up. "You nailed it. I'm impressed."

"Me, too," Millie said. "Excellent multi-tasking."

"Remembering names is what I do, but I've never tried it while line dancing."

"Hey, Jake." Rafe showed up with the blonde woman Nell could now identify as his wife Kate. "Way to put Nell on the spot, bro."

"Got the job done."

"And she handled it." Zeke slid his arm around her waist.

The gesture was lovely. The affection in his voice was even better. "And now I know everybody's name. Nice to meet you, Millie and Kate. I—"

"We'll be taking a short break, folks!" The lead singer's voice flowed from the speakers on the bandstand. "We'll be back after the cake."

Zeke frowned. "Cake?"

"Val told me Ben wheels out a huge chocolate cake with a candle for each year Harland's been principal."

"Here's an idea, Jake." Matt came over with Lucy. "We'll use this break to introduce our—oh, wait. You already did the complicated thing, instead."

"My idea was more fun."

"Way more." Nell sent him a smile. His creative effort said a lot about the guy. He clearly wanted her to feel welcome. She was growing fond of Zeke's big brother.

Zeke glanced at her. "You'll need to go back over to the table for the cake thing."

"Right." But it meant interrupting the dynamic she had going with Zeke and her new friends.

"After the break, we can—"

The squeal of a microphone preceded another announcement. "I've been told everybody's invited to have a piece of cake, including the band. And whoa, I can see why. That's one ginormous pastry. And a heck of a lot of candles! See you over there, folks."

"We get cake, too?" Nick stood on the fringes of the group, his arm around Eva, his fiancé. "We should come to this every year."

Rafe gave him a look. "So that we can pay our respects to Apple Grove's teachers, right, Nicholas?"

"Well, sure." Nick rubbed his flat stomach. "And help them eat that big ol' cake."

Nell laughed. "Then my all means, let's head over there." Easy to see why Claire talked about her aunts and uncles with such affection. They were a lovable bunch. Hanging out with Zeke came with several perks and the Buckskin gang was one of them.

9

Moments later, Zeke stood in line with Nell as Ben passed out generous slices of cake handed to him by a server. Zeke had met the Choosy Moose owner several times. A robust sixty-something, he had the same impressive silver mane as Zeke and Jake's father.

The resemblance ended there. Ben was a straight-shooter, a generous soul who'd started a Christmas toy drive for needy kids many years ago and it was still going strong. Ben also thought Henri Fox hung the moon. Zeke agreed with him.

When Nell stepped up to get her cake, Ben's face lit up. "You're the new teacher!"

"I am. But how did you know?"

"Claire showed me a picture she took with Zeke's phone when you were working on the greenhouse project. Awesome idea."

"Thank you. I couldn't have done it without this guy." She turned to Zeke with a smile. "And Claire. She was a big help, too."

"She loved that project," Ben said. "You weren't here for the Christmas party, right?"

"Didn't want to spread my germs."

"Good call. Nice to finally meet you." He took the next serving of cake and handed it to her. "You're gonna like this."

"I'm sure. Thanks for the party."

"My pleasure."

She stepped aside and Zeke moved forward.

"That's quite a cake, Ben."

"Wait'll you taste it."

"If it's as good as the slices I've ordered here before—"

"Even better. This one's got a mocha filling. If it's a hit, we'll add it to the menu." He handed Zeke his cake. "Looks like the whole gang is here except Leo and Fiona."

"They're spending a couple of weeks with Fiona's parents."

"Somehow I missed that memo, but I'm happy for them. I have a stake in that relationship."

"So I heard." Clearly matchmaking was a thing in Apple Grove and Claire fit right in. He thanked Ben for the cake and joined Nell on the sidelines. Her piece was untouched. "You don't like mocha with your chocolate?"

"I love that combo. I was waiting for you."

"That was sweet."

She gave him a flirty look. "I'm a sweet person."

"You'll get no argument from me." He picked up his fork. "Let's dig in." He cut into the cake but held off taking a bite so he could watch her reaction. If this was better than the kind he'd ordered here before, she'd be a happy lady.

She slid the fork into her mouth. Then she closed her eyes and moaned.

Look away, dude. But he didn't. And he paid for it. A surge of lust made him reconsider taking that bite. Choking would not be cool. "Like it?"

She chewed, swallowed and opened her eyes. "I *love* it." Pleasure put stars in her eyes. "If Ben adds it to the menu, I'd come back just for this." She forked up another bite and checked out his plate. "What are you waiting for?"

"Just having fun watching you enjoy yourself."

Her gaze met his. Slowly her cheeks turned pink and her lips parted.

He forgot all about cake. And the people gathered around them. And his vow not to get involved with her. He'd never been so desperate to kiss a woman in his life.

She sucked in a breath. "Um, we should—"

"Yes, ma'am." He blinked. "We should eat this. The band will be back any minute." He started in. The cake was rich and creamy, but no substitute for what he wanted.

Just when he needed willpower, it had deserted him. He planned to finish this cake and dance to as many fast tunes as Nell could handle. Maybe he'd work through his obsession with kissing her plump, rosy lips, which were currently flavored with mocha and chocolate. His jeans pinched.

Ben's voice came over the sound system. "There's more cake for anyone who wants a second piece."

Can I get it to go? Oh, boy, now he was projecting images on his fevered brain that would drive him crazy if he didn't shut them down ASAP. Tearing his gaze from Nell, he focused on Ben up at the mic.

"The band will return in about five minutes. Before they do, let's take this opportunity to thank Principal Kuhn and the faculty and staff of Apple Grove Elementary. They're doing a terrific job. Let's show 'em some love."

Zeke found a spot to put his plate so he could join in the standing ovation. Nell looked tickled by it. He wanted to give her a congratulatory hug. Did he dare? He hesitated a little too long.

"Be right back." She touched his arm. "Val and I are ducking into the restroom before the dancing starts again."

The second she was gone, the Buckskin gang descended on him with a chorus of *we told you so* and *now what?*

Zeke sighed. "I'll tell you what." He directed his comments at Jake, who was clearly the ringleader. "Nothing. We'll dance a few more dances and then I'll go home and she'll go home. Separately."

"That's not how it looks to the rest of us, little brother."

"And I guarantee that's not what she's expecting," Millie added. "I caught the hot look that passed between you two a bit ago. Add that to all the fancy dancing you two have been doing, and I figured you'd be driving her home. She's likely thinking the same."

"But you don't know that."

"No, I don't, but I'd bet my new set of porch rockers she and her friend are in the restroom discussing your intentions."

"I agree with Millie," Kate said. "If you don't drive her home, she'll be confused at the very least. That look you gave her was enough to singe her eyebrows."

Guilt slammed into him. "You make a good point. Maybe I should have a private talk with her, let her know where I stand."

"Like during the drive to her place?" Jake gave him a pointed look.

"I don't think that's a good idea."

Rafe weighed in. "It's the best you've got, buddy. You can't have that kind of discussion here, with all these folks around and music blaring. If you feel the need to explain yourself, take her home and do it on the way."

"And I'd leave soon if I were you," Garrett said. "The more time you spend dancing with her, the more you're leading her on. That's not fair."

"Okay, okay. I get it. One more dance, and I'll suggest driving her home. I'll tell her I need to explain my unique situation so she doesn't get the wrong idea."

Jake coughed. "Right. Do that. Good plan."

"Thanks."

"Can I see you privately for a minute? Before she gets back?"

"Okay." Zeke followed him over to the far corner of the room. "Look, I mean it. I don't have time for romance. I have to concentrate on Claire."

"Take a lesson from Nell. She knows how to multi-task."

"She's amazing. But I can't risk getting involved with her, Jake. Claire needs me."

His brother gazed at him. "You've managed to go dancing with us almost every week."

"No woman wants a guy who can only spare one night a week."

"Why assume that? Ask the lady. She might surprise you."

"I can't imagine asking her that."

Jake gazed at him. "All right, then don't." He reached in his pocket. "But in case the subject comes up, so to speak, take these."

"Good God, Jake."

"Take 'em."

"*No*." He glanced around. "I can't believe you have those handy. What the hell are you—"

"I brought them in anticipation of this very scenario. Unless you're a complete idiot, you'll put them in your pocket. A Lassiter does not go into the unknown unprepared."

"You made that up just now."

"I did, but I like it. Gonna remember it. Anyway, she never has to know you've got 'em. Unless..."

"It won't be happening."

"Then you can give them back tomorrow."

"Don't worry, I will." Zeke took the condoms and quickly shoved them in his pocket with a silent pledge that they'd stay there.

Well, unless he found a way to ask that million-dollar question.

10

"I say he's going to ask to drive you home." Val dried her hands on a paper towel.

"And I say he won't." Nell took the towel Val handed her. "You didn't hear what he said to me during the field trip."

"No, but I saw the smokin' hot way he looked at you while you were eating cake. He wants you bad."

"And he'll deny himself because he's convinced getting involved with a woman means short-changing Claire."

"I'll bet you a bottle of our favorite cab that he'll ask to take you home."

"Okay, sure." Nell wadded up the paper towel and tossed it in the trash. "It's a bet I'd love to lose."

As she and Val returned from the restroom, Zeke separated himself from the crowd surrounding the cake. "Would either of you like another slice? There's still plenty. I'd be happy to fetch you some."

Nell shook her head. "Thanks, but I'm on a sugar high from the first piece."

"Me, too," Val said, "but that's never stopped me before. I'll get my own, though. I happen to know Nell loves the song they just started playing. You two should dance."

Zeke sent Nell a questioning look.

"It's one of my favorites."

"Alrighty, then." He flashed a smile at Val. "If you'll excuse us."

"You bet." She winked at Nell.

Zeke guided her through the maze of tables as the lead singer crooned the opening lyrics of Faith Hill and Tim McGraw's duet *I Need You."*

"I didn't ask if you wanted more cake."

"I'd rather dance to one of your favorite songs." He stepped onto the floor and pulled her close, his gaze holding hers.

"Do you like it?"

"I do." He began a gentle two-step. No complicated moves. No fancy twirls as the words spilled around them, sliding into her heart.

One of the guitar players, a young woman with dark hair, joined the lead singer for the second half of the duet. Nell searched Zeke's expression and found warmth and caring. Banked passion. But sadness tinged the heat glowing in his dark eyes.

She'd win the bet with Val. He wanted her, and she'd cling to that. Despite her frustration, she admired his selfless dedication to Claire. If only he could expand his image of the future.

The sweet song drew to a soft close. He stopped moving. "I have a favor to ask."

"Oh?"

"I'm struggling with…"

"I know."

"I'd like to talk it out with you, if you'd be willing."

"All right." She glanced around. "I'm not sure where we—"

"Could I take you home? Not that I plan to stay. I just—"

"You can take me home." She let out a breath. A talk. "That would be nice." She wasn't pinning any hopes on the outcome, but at least they'd be alone for the first time ever. Having him all to herself, even for that ten-minute trip, would be something.

"Can we go now?"

"Absolutely." A jolt of anticipation made her light-headed, as if she'd chugged a glass of champagne. "I just need to grab my purse and let Val and the Kuhns know I won't be riding back with them."

"I'll go with you." A hand at her back, he started toward her seat.

"Don't you want to tell the Buckskin gang you're leaving? I can meet you at the door."

"They already know. They're the ones who suggested this."

"Oh." That made her smile. "Interesting."

"I'll explain once we're in the truck."

"Can't wait to hear all about it." Making her announcement to Val and the Kuhns as brief as possible, she avoided looking at Val. Her friend would draw the wrong conclusion, but so what?

Zeke added his goodbyes and they made their escape. When he held the door for her, she stepped into a night meant for lovers.

A slight breeze stirred air that neither warmed nor cooled her skin. Scented with the flowers blooming on the square, it caressed her with the light brush of a cat's paw. A crescent moon hovered overhead and the old-fashioned street lamps created puddles of light on the sidewalk.

"My truck's close." He kept his hand at the small of her back as he guided her away from the Moose.

"What a beautiful night."

"Sure is. My first summer here."

"Mine, too."

He slowed. "Here we are." He helped her into the truck, walked around the front and climbed behind the wheel.

When he closed the door, cocooning them in this intimate space, her body vibrated with tension. Not that it was a bad thing. She liked being tucked into a private venue with Zeke.

"Better get going." His voice sounded strained as he put his hat on the dash, shoved the keys in the ignition and started the truck.

It was an odd comment. They had no time constraints. He could drive to her place at five miles an hour and nobody would care. That said, urgency registered in every move he made.

"You have something to get off your chest."

"Yes, I do." Taking a cursory glance over his shoulder, he backed the truck out of the diagonal parking space and drove at a good clip toward the end of the block.

He didn't speak again until he made the right turn that would take him to the town's residential section. "Garrett pointed out that I haven't been fair to you, and he's right."

"I'm not sure what you mean." Not quite true. But she wanted more than vague generalizations.

"I've told you I wouldn't date because of my obligations to Claire. Tonight I... sent a different signal."

"Yes."

He cleared his throat and gripped the wheel tighter. "I apologize."

"For what?"

"Dancing with you so often."

"I can't speak for you, but I had fun."

"So did I. That's the problem."

"Why?"

"I think you know why."

Uh-uh. You're not dodging that question, buddy. "I'm not sure I do." A quick glance confirmed his jaw was clenched.

Silence. Then finally, as if forcing them out, he said the words. "Because I want you."

Okay! She opened her mouth to respond.

"I've wanted you for some time."

Whoa. Let the man talk.

"I've done my best to hide it. Until tonight. I got carried away and likely gave you the wrong impression. You probably thought I'd changed my mind but I haven't."

"I know that you—"

"Claire is my priority. She comes first and that will never change. I'm a full-time dad, which means I can't be leaving her with babysitters all the time. That's—"

"Look, I underst—"

"Jake thinks you might be fine with only getting together one night a week, but I—"

"What?"

"I can't imagine asking—"

"Are you saying you'd be okay with getting involved if it's only one night a week?" She was so shocked her voice squeaked.

"See?" He looked over at her. "You're insulted, right? You think that's cheesy."

"No, damn it! I think it's fabulous!"

"Huh?"

"It's a brilliant idea! Jake's a genius, and... you just drove past my house."

He slammed on the brakes and turned to her, disbelief etched in his face and every line of his taut body. "You're kidding."

"No." She gasped for breath.

"You wouldn't feel cheated?"

"As opposed to never making love to you?" She put a hand to her chest where her heart was banging so hard it physically hurt. "Are you crazy?"

"Evidently." He put the truck in reverse, backed down the street and swerved into a spot next to the curb in front of her bungalow. Then he shut off the motor and looked over at her, his chest heaving. "Claire's at Henri's for the night."

She swallowed. "Would you like to come in?"

"I would, and..." He took a shaky breath. "I never expected this to happen."

"I believe you. And you're not prepared. Neither am I. But we—"

"Except I am prepared."

"You are? Why?"

"Turns out Jake brought—"

"Oh, my God." She clapped a hand to her mouth and started to giggle.

"I told him no, but he insisted so I had to take them before someone noticed. I mean, there we were, with people all around, and he's pulling condoms out of his pocket. What was I supposed to do?"

"Oh, Zeke." She gulped and wiped her eyes. "Your brother's awesome."

"Yes, ma'am." He smiled. "Let's go inside."

_11_

By the time Zeke made it around the truck, Nell had opened the door and started down. "Let me." He moved in. Somehow the process of helping her out turned into pulling her close. "I have to kiss you."

"Great, because I have to kiss you, too." She met him halfway, her gaze eager, her arms sliding around his neck.

With a groan, he tasted lips he'd craved since the first day of building that greenhouse. Velvety soft and supple, they welcomed him with enthusiasm. Oh, God, this was going to be good.

His heart hammered as she pressed her body against his. With a soft moan, she invited him to go deeper. He accepted. Delving into her hot mouth aroused him so fast he gasped at the surge of his cock against the barrier of his jeans.

She eased back just a little, her breath warm on his mouth, her voice husky. "I think we'd better go in."

"I think you're right."

Draping his arm around her shoulders, he drew her away from the truck and pushed the door shut. "Let's go."

"Let's hurry."

He chuckled. "Let's not."

"Oh." She wrapped her arm around his waist as they started up the walk. "Maybe that kiss wasn't such a good idea."

"Like I could have helped myself."

"Like I could have, either."

"Longest front walk in the world."

"Almost there."

"Got your key?"

"In a sec." She fumbled with the little purse hanging by a strap from her shoulder. "I'm shaking."

"That makes two of us."

"Got it." She fished out her keyring.

"So many keys."

"Mine plus the ones for school." She took a breath. "When we worked on the project, did you—"

"Think about this? Yes, ma'am." He climbed the steps to the porch, matching his stride to hers. A lamp in the window cast a soft glow. "From day one. How about you?"

"Since you walked into my classroom with Claire." She twisted the key in the lock, pushed on the door and pulled him inside. "And now I have you right where I want you."

"That goes both ways." He started to tug her closer.

"Not yet." She backed away. "If you kiss me here, we'll never make it to my bedroom."

"Then lead on, pretty lady." He followed her into a room with a bed and a lamp to see her by. All he needed. "I'm kissing you, now."

"Please do." She moved into his arms and lifted her face to his. "Everywhere."

He gulped, his hand trembling as he cupped her cheek. "You're blushing."

"I'm blushing all over."

"God, Nell." He captured her mouth and tightened his grip on her waist, aligning her hips with his, pressing his aching body against the softness of her breasts and the inviting cleft between her thighs. His heartbeat thudded in his ears, making him dizzy.

He thrust his tongue into her mouth and she whimpered. Cupping his glutes, she urged him closer, wiggling into position so he was... *right there.*

Gasping, he lifted his head. "I can't... I need..."

"Me, too." She broke away from him, clutched her blouse and pulled it over her head.

Okay, then. He began shucking his clothes, not caring where they went as he kept his gaze on her. When she stripped off her underwear, he went still, fighting for control as a tidal wave of desire threatened to knock him over.

"Look at you." He swallowed. "Look at you! You're... you're perfect."

She flushed a rosy pink. The color touched her cheeks, highlighting the happy sparkle in her eyes. Then it moved past her smiling lips to her graceful throat and spread over her plump breasts. Moisture pooled in his mouth as her nipples tightened.

She'd asked him to kiss her everywhere. He would. Oh, yes, he would, but not now, not when

the ache of an impending climax told him he was
running out of time.

He stumbled backward and clenched his
hands to keep from grabbing her. Sure, he'd been
out of the game for a while, but that didn't explain
his overpowering urge to unzip and make the
ultimate connection. The sooner, the better.

But this wasn't just about sex. It was about
Nell. Ah, how she tempted him, from the curve of
her narrow waist to the flair of her hips and the lure
of her creamy thighs. He wanted... God, how he
wanted.

His gaze returned to lock with hers.
"Seems you do." His voice sounded like someone
raking gravel.

"Do what?"

"Blush all over."

She glanced down and her breath hitched.
"Guess so." She looked up again. "I'm feeling a little
shaky. Think I'll lie down."

"Think I'll join you." Chest heaving, he
went back to undressing, fumbling in his haste.
Anyone would think he'd never done this before.

Then again, he hadn't. Not with Nell. It was
shaping up to be a game changer. She lay on her
side, shallow breathing, her head propped on her
hand.

He couldn't stop looking at her. Pulling the
condoms out of his jeans pocket, he tossed them on
the bedside table.

She glanced at them briefly, smiled, and
returned her attention immediately to him. When
he shucked his jeans and briefs in one go, her lips
parted and her blush deepened.

If the sight of his body caused a reaction in her that was anything like the way she stirred him, they were in for an explosion. He reached for a condom, tore open the package and rolled it on.

She didn't miss a single second of that. Her breathing was faster, now, and the light in her eyes beckoned him. She didn't say a word. Didn't have to. Rolling to her back, she spread her thighs and opened her arms.

Their communication had moved to the realm of touch. Pulled by the force of her gaze and the invitation of her body, he settled between her thighs and flattened his palms on either side of her head.

Holding his gaze, she wrapped her arms around him, fingers kneading the tight muscles of his back. He leaned down and captured her mouth, taking the kiss deep, claiming her with his tongue.

She moved her grip lower and pressed her fingers into his glutes, a clear signal. An urgent request.

He lowered his hips. She lifted hers. Guided by an age-old instinct, he plunged into her quivering channel. She met that first thrust with a climax that rolled over his cock, undulating around him in waves of ecstasy.

He lost what was left of his mind. Wrenching his mouth from hers, he pounded into her, taking her up again and gasping as her muscles contracted around him and she clutched his glutes, pulling him in tight, shuddering beneath him. She yelled this time, and so did he. So close.

But somehow he hung on for one more wild sprint to the finish. The room filled with their labored breathing and the liquid sounds of two bodies coming together with enough force to send the headboard slamming against the wall.

When she cried out a third time, he abandoned himself to the rush of an orgasm that roared through him with the energy of a flash flood, sweeping away every rational thought but one. *It had never been like this.*

Eventually the room stopped spinning. Gradually his lungs had enough air to allow him to speak. She hadn't said anything yet, likely because she was dazed and wiped out, too.

He glanced down. Nope, not dazed. Instead she was grinning, her eyes dancing with laughter. "And you were ready to give this up."

"Because I'm an idiot?"

"Yes!" She pinched his butt. "All that sexual energy and you were prepared to keep it bottled up indefinitely. I predict that sooner or later you would have exploded."

"I think I just did."

"We both did. I could blame those rapid-fire orgasms on my nun-like existence this past year, but I don't think that's it. I think it's you."

"I'm not taking all the credit. You were on fire before I ever joined the party."

"That was all you. I almost came watching you take off your clothes."

"That's hard to believe."

"Have you looked in a mirror lately? Checked out your pecs and abs?"

"Just so you know, that's not a thing I do."

"So you're not vain. I like that, actually. But take my word for it, you have impressive muscles.

When you unveiled the rest of the goodies, you put me right on the edge."

"Surprised the heck out of me when you came so fast. Made me go a little crazy, to be honest."

"Which made me go even crazier. I've never had multis."

"Never?"

"You're the first. It's a little scary, getting off to such a great start." She laughed. "What if we've hit our peak and it's all downhill from here?"

"You don't believe that."

"No, I don't. I believe we're in for a whole lot of fun."

His chest tightened. She was so generous. "Thank you, Nell."

She reached up and stroked his cheek. "Feeling grateful?"

"Very." He kissed her gently. "And I hope you're not sleepy, because I'd like to express my gratitude a few more times before I go home."

"Can't wait."

_12_

Nell enjoyed more fabulous lovemaking in the next few hours than she'd experienced in her entire adult life. Zeke left at five because he was on barn duty. She suffered guilt pangs because he'd had so little sleep, but that didn't stop her from going back to bed and conking out for several hours.

When she woke up, she found a text from Zeke on her phone. _You're amazing. See you tomorrow._

She texted back. _Looking forward to it._ Then she texted Valerie and arranged to meet her for coffee at Cup of Cheer when it opened at eleven. She ate a quick breakfast, showered and dressed in jeans and a T-shirt.

She'd overdone it with Zeke and was tender in some intimate spots. Who cared? She had a week to recover before they'd do it all over again next weekend, either Friday or Saturday night. He would let her know when the gang was heading back to the Moose.

The square was quiet on a Sunday morning. Summer had arrived, bringing with it lush green grass to showcase the freshly painted white gazebo. The cheerful border of flowers surrounding the base of it matched her mood. She grabbed a diagonal parking spot in front of Cup of Cheer, one of the few businesses open.

Val had arrived at the coffee shop ahead of her and had snagged a two-top beside the large window that looked out on the square. She glanced up when Nell approached the table, a wine bag in hand.

Nell did her best to play it cool. "You win, since he asked to drive me home. I happened to have a bottle on hand, so here you go." She set the bag on the table.

"*And?*"

Nell grinned. "He left at five this morning."

"Oh, my *God.* Sit down this minute. Tell me everything."

"Well, that's not gonna happen." She laughed when Val made a face. "I'll tell you what led up to his decision to stay, though."

"And maybe a few tiny details? I'm living vicariously through you."

"Some broad brush strokes, then. Let me place our order first. What do you want? My treat."

"The Summer Lovin' special brew and a cheese Danish, please."

"Be right back." She went up to the counter and wasn't surprised Isabel wasn't there taking orders. Her employees usually handled the light Sunday crowd. After placing the order, she returned to the table and took a seat across from Val.

Her phone pinged. "Excuse me a minute." She glanced at her phone. A smiley face emoji blowing a kiss. Excitement curled in her stomach.

"Whatever went on last night must have been good, because you look like a kid with a handful of tickets for the Tilt-a-Whirl. And you're blushing."

"That's it in a nutshell. Couldn't have said it better."

"Was that him texting you?"

"Yes."

"Are you seeing him again tonight?"

"No." She explained the arrangement they'd made.

"I take it you're fine with that."

"Like I told him, something's better than nothing. And we're so good together. We—"

"*Good*? Is that code for off-the-charts sex?"

Nell's cheeks warmed. "Yeah."

"Awesome. It's a shame you're limited to once-a-week, though."

"If last night's an example, I'll need the time to recover."

Val groaned. "You're killing me, girlfriend. Did I happen to mention that I've spent the school year living in the same state of nunnery as you? Am I allowed to be jealous as hell?"

"Listen, come to the Moose with us next time the Buckskin gang goes. Maybe you'll—"

"The Brotherhood is a swoony bunch, but they're all spoken for."

"I'm not talking about them. I'm just saying it's a chance to meet single guys, and if you like cowboys, they usually hang out there, and—"

"Thanks for the invitation. I'll definitely think about it."

"You should. If nothing else, you'd get the opportunity to dance, even if nobody suits you. And you'd get to know the Brotherhood. You'd love those guys. They're so...."

"Hot?"

"Well, yeah, but they're also genuine."

"Hot and genuine." Val sighed. "I need to find me one of those."

"I was lucky. If Claire had been a different age, I might never have met Zeke. He's such an amazing dad. I love the way he and Claire interact. He—"

"So it's his parenting skills that hooked you in?" Val had a teasing gleam in her eyes.

She laughed. "At first. But now that I know him better, I wouldn't say that's the big draw."

"Can't wait to hear what the *big draw* is."

"That's not up for discussion."

"Just so it's *up* when you—"

"*Val.*" She ducked her head and grabbed a napkin to muffle her whoop of laughter. "Stop."

"I made you blush again. I'm guessing he was all you'd hoped for and more."

"I'm not answering that."

"You don't have to. You're glowing."

"I've never met anyone like him. But then I've never dated anyone who had a kid. Watching his loving behavior with Claire adds a new dimension. I like it."

"I'm happy that you're happy. Me, I'm not looking for that situation. A little too domestic for me. I just want someone to have fun with. And not to change the subject, but we need to decide who's driving tomorrow. I can, but it'll be a tight fit. The back seat of my truck is tiny."

"Then let's just take my SUV. It has plenty of room."

"I was hoping you'd offer. But I've always wondered why you traded your sports car for that big old SUV instead of a snazzy little truck."

"I looked at ones like yours, but I wanted more flexibility."

"For when you have kids?"

"Not really." She shrugged. "I was over the tiny sports car that only held two people and wasn't good in the snow."

"I get that. And I'm grateful you have it to ferry us out to the Buckskin this summer. I'll cover the gas."

"Never mind about the gas. You can provide wine for happy hour after the girls go home. Seeing Zeke tomorrow and trying to pretend nothing's changed will be weird. After we get back and send the kids home, I'd love to order a pizza, drink wine and decompress."

"I'm in. Do you think Claire will pick up on the new status quo?"

"I'll be amazed if she doesn't. She might not know exactly what's going on, but she'll know something's different."

"And I'll have a ringside seat to watch her reaction. And his. And yours. Exciting stuff. It'll be a miracle if I manage to concentrate on the business at hand with all that going on."

Nell gazed at her. "I'll be in the same boat, girlfriend."

13

"Are you okay, Dad?"

"I'm great, Claire." Zeke ducked under Prince's belly and grabbed the cinch. "This'll be lots of fun. Looking forward to it." Which he was. He was as eager and excited as his daughter, but for very different reasons.

"I just wondered." She pulled Lucky's cinch tight. "You keep dropping things. That's not like you."

"Probably drank too much coffee today."

"*Again*? Yesterday you drank coffee like it was going out of style. That's not good for you."

"You're right, sweetie. I'll cut back." Yesterday's coffee had been a lifesaver. As had Garrett, who'd spent his day off with Anna and little Georgie. He'd invited Claire to hang out with them, leaving her little time to quiz her exhausted dad about his night at the Moose and the Apple Grove faculty party. He owed Garrett.

Claire slipped Lucky's bridle in place. "I looked up the dangers and benefits of coffee, and three cups is plenty."

"I'll keep that in mind." Excess caffeine wasn't his problem. Was that the purr of an engine?

Yep, sure was. His heart pumped faster and sweat trickled down his backbone, even though a few clouds and a cooling trend had banished the heat.

"I hear a car! Hey, Lucky, they're coming down the road, big boy. I told them to bring carrots, and they—"

"Not too many, I hope?"

"No, Dad." She rolled her eyes. "I told them to bring just what you said."

"Thanks." She was calling him *dad* more often these days.

"You asked me about the carrots an hour ago."

"I did?"

"Yes, and that's the other thing. You're repeating yourself. Something's making you distracted. You were like that yesterday, too. Loopy."

"Like I said, too much caffeine. I promise to limit myself."

"Good. Oh, boy, here they come! Lucky, you are going to *love* helping my friends learn how to ride. And Miss O'Connor and Miss Jenson, too. You'll be their hero."

"How about Prince, Butch and Sundance?" If he kept talking, maybe his attack of nerves would pass. "Won't they be heroes, too?" He picked up Prince's halter from the hitching post. Nell's SUV pulled in and he dropped the halter.

"Dad. You're doing it again."

"I know." He scooped it up and shook off the dirt.

"I hope you don't have a condition."

He choked back a laugh. He had a condition, all right. The cause had just climbed out of the driver's side of that SUV.

She was mostly hidden by the vehicle and the luggage rack on top of it. He could see her baseball cap bobbing around as she opened the back door. Her hair must be stuffed under it. A few dark strands had escaped. He'd never forget how she looked with those glossy curls spread across the pillow...

"Dad."

He blinked. "What?"

"You might need a checkup. I think you're going deaf, too."

"No, I'm not."

"Then what did I just say?"

"You said something?"

"*Ye*-es. I said we should go meet them."

"Good idea." He set the halter back on the hitching post and put a hand on her shoulder. "No running or shouting."

"I know. Before we left school on Thursday, Miss O'Connor had a talk with us about not freaking out the horses. We promised to hold it down, even though we're super excited to see each other."

"You saw each other four days ago."

"That's a long time when you care about somebody."

Tell me about it. Since he'd left Nell yesterday morning, the hours had inched by at the speed of a geriatric turtle. When he glimpsed her smiling face, *he* wanted to run and shout. And hug and kiss. Not happening. Not until Friday night, a lifetime away.

She walked toward him with one hand on Riley's shoulder and the other on Tatum's. "Hello, Mr. Lassiter."

"Hello, Miss O'Connor." In addition to the San Francisco Giants baseball cap, she wore sunglasses. No fair. He wanted to look into her eyes. His hungry gaze moved lower.

Her Apple Grove Cougars T-shirt was boxy and loose, unlike the low-cut top she'd had on Saturday night. But her jeans were snug enough to make his breath hitch. He'd never seen her in boots, but she had them on today. No wonder she looked a little taller.

And, oh, by the way, he was staring. Not good. He focused on Valerie, who had her hand on Piper's shoulder. "Miss Jenson, nice to see you again."

"Same here, Mr. Lassiter." Valerie's outfit matched Nell's except for the hat. Her straw Stetson was almost as beat-up as his. She flashed him a knowing grin.

Oh, right. Nell would have filled her in on Saturday night's proceedings. He flushed and switched his attention to Piper, Riley and Tatum. Focusing on those girls settled him down immediately.

He had the privilege of giving Piper and Tatum their first horseback riding experience. Riley would only watch, but she'd be soaking up everything he told the other two. They were three sponges, just like Claire, and he was responsible for the quality of what they absorbed. He took that seriously.

They were beside themselves, stars in their eyes and smiles that took over their rosy-cheeked faces. Was Claire their fashion consultant? Could be, since they all had hats like hers, Roper boots, yoked shirts in different colors and Wrangler jeans. Mini-cowgirls, ready to ride.

His heart squeezed. "Riley, Tatum, Piper— I'm so glad you're here."

"Me, too!" Claire gave a little bounce of joy. "I'm glad Miss O'Connor and Miss Jenson are here, too."

"So am I." He let his gaze rest on Nell for a second before turning to Valerie. "As you can see, I got the go-ahead for two more horses. I'll put Tatum and Piper on Lucky and Prince, and you two on Butch and Sundance."

Valerie nodded. "Sounds perfect."

"What should I do, Mr. Lassiter?" Riley turned her freckled face up to his.

"You'll be with me and Claire. Once everyone's mounted, you can help lead them into the corral. Then you and Claire will sit on the fence with me and be my assistant observers."

"Yes, sir!"

He tugged on his straw hat. "Piper and Tatum, your hats look terrific, but you'll need to trade them for helmets before you get on those horses."

"Awww." Tatum made a face.

"Told you," Claire said. "I have to wear one when I ride."

Riley nodded. "Me, too. Before I got my horse, my folks made me promise I'd wear one."

"What about us?" Valerie thumbed back her straw hat.

He grinned. He'd bet she'd been waiting to execute that move. "Since you're an adult, you can opt out of the helmet, but you'll have to sign a waiver."

"We'll wear the helmets." Nell glanced at her friend. "Right?"

"Oh, absolutely. It's the responsible thing to do."

"Hey, Dad, you could take a picture of me and my friends with our hats on before Piper and Tatum have to take theirs off."

"I could." He pulled his phone out of his pocket. "Scooch together." He crouched down. "Smile!" He took the picture and glanced at the screen. "Perfect."

"Let me see." Claire hurried around to look. "Cute. Now let me take one of you, Miss O'Connor and Miss Jenson. You should be in the middle."

Easier to agree than argue. He handed her the phone and walked over to stand between Nell and Valerie."

"Get closer. Put your arm around their waists, Dad. That'll look better."

He sucked in a breath and did as she asked. Both ladies were warm to the touch but Nell made his entire left side and left arm tingle as if he'd touched a live wire. He let go the minute Claire took the picture, his mouth dry and his heart going a mile-a-minute.

He held out his hand. "I'll take my phone back, now."

"Yes, sir." Claire exchanged a sly glance with Riley.

"Would you and Riley please go open the corral gate so it's ready for us?"

"Yes, sir." The two girls walked away, giggling.

Something had them going, but he'd be wise to ignore it. He led the procession over to the hitching post. "The horses are patiently waiting for us. Correction. Prince, Butch and Sundance are being patient. Lucky is dozing. He loves his naps. Have you two agreed on which horse you want?"

"Lucky!" they said together.

"Looks like we'll be drawing straws, then." Leaning down, he picked up a couple of stray bits of straw from the ground and went through the ritual with them. Piper got the long straw and Tatum was a good sport about it.

He turned to Nell and Valerie. "Do either of you have a preference?"

Nell took off her cap and sunglasses. "Are they named for the characters in that old movie with Newman and Redford?"

"Yes, ma'am. Charley, Henri's husband, had a fondness for it."

"Well, since I've always been a Paul Newman fan, I'd like to take Butch."

"Works for me," Valerie said. "I'm Team Redford."

"Alrighty, then. I'll take everyone's hats and stick 'em in the barn. I'll be right back with your helmets." A moment later he'd just finished distributing the helmets and was helping the girls put theirs on when Claire arrived with Riley close behind.

"Dad." She sounded out of breath.

"Something wrong?"

She let out a dramatic sigh. "Wouldn't you know, there's a *snake* in the corral."

Riley spread her arms wide. "A *big* snake."

"Rattler?"

Claire nodded. "We saw the tail."

"No problem. Everyone wait here. I'll just get a rake and move it."

Nell finished buckling her helmet and stepped forward. "I want to go with you."

He turned to stare at her. "Why?"

"I've never seen one and I'm curious." She looked at Piper and Tatum. "Have either of you seen one?"

They shook their heads.

"Want to?"

"Yes." Piper's jaw tightened and her eyes gleamed with determination. "Claire and Riley saw it. We want to see it, too, right, Tatum?"

"Right."

"That's the spirit." Nell glanced at Valerie. "How about you?"

"I've had the pleasure. I'll stay here and hold the horses."

"They won't go anywhere, Miss Jenson," Claire said. "You can come."

"Thanks, but I'll take a pass."

"Zeke, I'd like to take Tatum and Piper over there. It would be educational for the three of us to get a look."

"I hadn't thought of it that way. That's fine. Just let me go get the rake." Nell's suggestion had caught him by surprise. Plenty of folks were leery of rattlers. She might be, too, but evidently she couldn't resist the chance to educate herself and two girls she'd recently had in class.

He was damned impressed with this woman. What he wouldn't give to be able to hug her and tell her so. The effects of their slight contact during the picture-taking lingered. Friday couldn't come soon enough.

14

Nell put herself in charge of keeping the girls outside the corral and away from the gate while Zeke did his snake-charmer routine. Her urban childhood hadn't prepared her for encountering snakes in the wild, but she lived in Montana, now. She needed to learn about them and so did Piper and Tatum.

Her determination to maintain scientific detachment faltered as Zeke approached the snake armed only with a rake. A distinctly triangular head lifted to gaze at him, tongue darting out.

Piper sucked in a breath. "Ooo, your daddy's brave, Claire."

"Yep. I've seen him do this once before. The other snake was smaller."

"Good grief, that *is* a big dude." Valerie came up behind them.

"I thought you were holding the horses." Nell kept her attention on Zeke as he scooted the rake slowly toward the rattler.

"I was feeling like the Cowardly Lion while you guys were over here being all Dorothy and the Tin Man."

Tatum giggled. "You're funny, Miss Jenson."

"Funny and *very* brave." Nell glanced back over her shoulder.

"Thank you. How do I look in my helmet?"

"Stunning." She returned to watching Zeke.

"When we had a snake by our house," Riley said, "my mom used this pole with a loop on the end to pick it up and put it in a bucket with a lid."

"We have one of those." Claire kept her gaze on her father. "But a rake works, too. My dad grabs whatever's handy."

"That snake sure is watching him," Piper said.

"They're watching each other, sizing each other up." Claire sounded like the announcer at a sporting event. "My dad says snakes are necessary and we should respect them."

"I agree," Nell said. "Live and let live." And she hoped to hell Zeke knew what he was doing. Looked like it. She held her breath as the snake wound itself around the teeth and handle of the rake.

Lifting the rake, Zeke came quickly through the gate, biceps bulging. "She's a heavy one, too." He lengthened his stride as he moved past the barn and out into an open area.

Tatum stood on tiptoe. "Where's he taking it?"

"See that jumble of rocks?" Claire pointed to an area about fifty yards away. "He'll put it down out there. That's where he took the other one. They like rocks."

Piper turned to Claire. "Is that snake a girl? Is that why he said *she*?"

"Probably. Girl snakes are bigger than boy snakes."

"You're not scared of them?"

"I was a little bit with the first one. Then Dad showed me some documentaries that talked about how important snakes are. And I saw a few other kinds around here. When this one showed up, I wasn't scared at all."

Riley gave her a nudge. "Come on. You jumped back and grabbed my arm. You were a little scared."

"Not as much as *you*."

"It was a big snake. I mean *she* was a big snake."

"I'm glad she came to visit," Nell said. "It was a—"

"I know what you're gonna say, Miss O'Connor!" Claire beamed at her.

"What am I going to say?"

"It was a teachable moment."

She laughed. "Well, it was."

"She says that all the time, Miss Jenson." Claire glanced at Valerie. "Like at least once a day."

"I see." Val nodded. "Then you must have learned a lot this past year."

"We actually did." Piper adjusted her glasses. "Third grade was my favorite so far. Especially the greenhouse."

"Yeah, that was awesome." Tatum danced a little. "But the field trip was the best. Do we get a field trip in fourth grade, Miss Jenson?"

"Um... yes, yes, you do."

"Cool!" Riley twirled around. "Where to?"

"I'm keeping that a secret."

Nell managed not to laugh. Quite likely Val didn't have one planned yet.

"Miss Snake is back where she belongs." Zeke arrived, the rake balanced over his shoulder. "Time to saddle up."

"Yay!" Tatum started off at a run.

"Walk!" Nell's command brought Tatum to a screeching halt as she waited for the others. As the group started off again, the other three teased her for running ahead.

"Nell, I'll see you and Val over there." Zeke lengthened his stride to catch up to the girls. "I'll put Tatum and Piper on first."

"Nice job with the snake," Nell called after him.

"Thanks." He flashed her a grin over his shoulder.

"A greenhouse and a field trip to this ranch." Val chuckled. "You'll be a tough act to follow. I'd better be at the top of my game."

"No worries. They'll bring out the best in you. It was a blast teaching them."

"I'll tell you who's already at the top of his game." She tilted her head in the direction of Zeke as he walked with four adoring little girls, two on either side. "He's a natural with kids."

"I figured that out during the field trip. Don't you just want to eat him up with a spoon?" She watched as the girls skipped along beside him, chattering away.

"I'll neither confirm nor deny. A friend does not covet her friend's man."

"You can still agree with me that he's appealing as hell—all those muscles and a nurturer, to boot."

He stood talking to the girls for a moment. Then he used his cupped hands to give Tatum a place for her foot as she mounted Prince. He did the same for Piper.

Val moved off to the side and kept her voice down. "Since he's a nurturer, do you suppose he wants more than one kid?"

"Maybe." *I hope so.* Yikes, where had that come from? Fantasizing about having Zeke's baby was way off-base. "Claire said she pretends the three-year-old who lives on the ranch is her little brother."

"Georgie? The one she was talking about in the car on the way here?"

"Uh-huh." Judging from Claire's comments, she'd spent most of Sunday with Georgie, Garrett and Anna. Nell was willing to bet Garrett had set that up to give Zeke a break since he'd had so little sleep.

He'd likely be sleep-deprived again this weekend. "By the way, Zeke texted me this morning. The Buckskin gang's heading to the Moose Friday night. You're invited. We can pick you up."

"I'd better drive myself."

"That's silly. We can—"

"Once I get there, I'd like to stay a while." She grinned. "I doubt you and Zeke will last longer than one dance."

Nell flushed. "No, we're going to hang out with everybody."

"Sure you are."

"Val, we like dancing and spending time with the Buckskin gang. This is about more than getting horizontal."

"Of course it is, but after exercising restraint all week, you'll be a couple of powder kegs."

An excellent description of her condition right now. "Change the subject, please." She took a deep breath as Claire walked in their direction.

"Dad says to come on over. He's ready to get you up on Butch and Sundance."

She nodded. "Okay."

Claire glanced up at her. "Did you bring any water, Miss O'Connor?"

"I have a water bottle for each of us in the car, but I wasn't sure when—"

"Maybe you should go fetch them before you get on Butch. You look a little overheated."

A muffled snort from Val was followed by elaborate throat-clearing. "We probably should do that, Miss O'Connor." Her voice quivered with suppressed laughter. "Wouldn't want you to get too hot."

15

When Claire informed Zeke that Nell and Valerie were going to fetch water bottles for themselves and the girls, he ducked his head to hide a smile. Most likely they needed time to recover from their laughing fit. If he had to guess, he'd say the hilarity had to do with him.

If any of the Brotherhood were around, they'd probably be laughing, too. His preoccupation with Nell had to be blindingly obvious.

He glanced at Piper and Tatum. "While they're fetching the water bottles, we can go over the basics of neck reining. It's the same idea as when you nudge a friend to get her to go in the direction you want. Only instead you lay the reins against the horse's neck—on the left side to nudge them right and on the right side to nudge them left."

Riley nodded. "I do that with Mister Rogers."

"Your riding coach?"

"My horse. The person who named him loved that show. She was hoping he would be gentle like the guy on the show, and he is."

"Sounds like you got a great horse, Riley."

Her face lit up. "I sure did." She twirled around. "Wish you could see him."

"*I've* seen him," Tatum said. "He's a nice brown color like Lucky. You should just ride him over here."

"I'm not allowed to go on the road, but we have a horse trailer. Maybe..." She stood still, head cocked, expression intent. Then she gave a quick nod. "I'm gonna ask. They wouldn't bring him every time, but maybe just once, as a special treat. Then me and Mister Rogers could ride with you guys."

"Dad! I just had the best idea. At the last riding lesson in August, we should put on a demonstration for the parents and... anybody who wants to come. Riley can bring Mister Rogers and we can all be on horseback, even you. Wouldn't that be cool?"

"Oh, yeah!" Tatum bounced a little in the saddle. "Let's do that, Mr. Lassiter!"

"We'll see." He glanced at the shyest one of the bunch. "Do you want to do something like that, Piper?"

"Yes, sir. As long as I can ride Lucky."

"He's all yours," Tatum said. "I've decided I like buckskins the best. I'm going to get one someday."

"Then I'll ask Mrs. Fox. She has the final word."

"Gramma Henri will *love* the idea. She'll invite the Babes. It should be on a Saturday, so everybody's free. We can—"

"They're coming back," Riley announced. "Can we tell them? I know it's not for sure, but—"

"You can tell them." As if he could keep something like this quiet. "Just be sure to add that I haven't asked my boss yet." Henri would green light this in a heartbeat, too. He'd quickly learned that she loved nothing better than a celebration.

Nell and Valerie were met with a barrage of excited chatter as the girls talked over each other in their excitement.

"Okay, okay." Nell held up both hands, palms out. "It's a fabulous idea and if Mrs. Fox is on board, then so am I. But if we don't stop gabbing and get busy, we won't have much to show the audience at the end of the summer, will we?"

The girls all nodded and order was restored.

Nell handed aluminum water bottles up to Tatum and Piper, one blue and one green. Then she gave Riley a red one.

"You remembered our favorite colors." Riley gave her a smile.

"I did. These can last you all summer. Claire, I have a purple one in here for you."

"Awesome! Thanks."

"Miss Jenson?" Nell held out the bag. "You get to pick from what's left."

"Oh, the orange one, for sure."

"Then I'll take yellow." She pulled it out. "Mr. Lassiter? I have one more."

"Sure. Thanks."

She gave him the last one, a bright pink. The girls started to giggle.

He met her amused gaze. "Much obliged." He took it, popped open the cap and took a long swallow.

"I'll be in charge of them for the duration." Her eyes sparkled. "After the lesson, I'll take them home, wash them and bring them back full. Just remember your color."

He lifted his in a toast. "Yes, ma'am. I'm not likely to forget mine."

After the water break, he explained neck reining to Nell and Valerie while Claire collected the bottles and carried the tote into the barn for safekeeping.

"Got it." Valerie walked over to Sundance and stroked his muzzle. "I'm ready to climb on my trusty steed, Mr. Lassiter. Did you say we get on from the left?"

"Yes, ma'am. Need help?"

"I watched the girls. I'd like to try it on my own."

"Then have at it." He turned to Nell, who was about four or five inches shorter than Valerie and might have trouble getting her foot in the stirrup. "Would you like me to help you up like I did the girls?"

"Thanks, but no thanks." She flashed him a grin. "If Val can do it, I can do it."

"Then by all means, go right ahead." She sounded like her eight-year-old charges just then. Cute.

She had to lift her foot high to reach the stirrup, but she managed it. With a little hop and a firm grip on the saddle horn, she hoisted herself aboard and grinned in triumph. "Knew I could."

"Well done."

Claire emerged from the barn. "Hey, Dad, can Riley and me lead Prince and Lucky into the corral?"

"You can, but then I want you to wait there until I bring the ladies in."

"Yes, sir. Come on, Riley."

"Go slow, sweetie." He'd spent three months teaching her safe methods for dealing with these large animals. He didn't need to remind her to take it easy. But he did, anyway. Habit.

She smiled, her expression adorably tolerant. "Yes, sir."

He turned back to Valerie. "Let's see if those stirrups are the right length. Put your weight on the balls of your feet and stand up." When she lifted from the saddle, he nodded. "Looks good."

He swung around toward Nell. "I need you to do the same." He gave her a clinical once-over. Yeah, right. Nothing clinical about checking out the fit of her jeans. "Your stirrups are too short. Slip your feet out and I'll lengthen them." He leaned in and pretended Nell was a stranger, a ranch guest, anybody other than the woman who'd writhed naked beneath him less than two days ago.

"Sundance and I will wander off a bit to give you two some privacy. I'll test out this neck-reining thing."

He glanced over his shoulder. "Hang on, Val. We'll be done in a sec." Or they would if he wasn't fumble-fingers as he adjusted the left stirrup.

"Take your time." She made a soft clucking sound and moved Sundance a few feet away.

Nell laughed. "Where'd you learn to make that noise, Val?"

"It's what the cowboys do in the movies. Turns out it works. So does neck-reining. Maybe this is my jam, after all."

"Could be, girlfriend. Could be."

Nell sounded relaxed, but he sure as hell wasn't. Not with her thigh inches from his face. He breathed in, hungry for the sweet scent of her.

Bad move. That delicious aroma delivered a message straight to his privates. He held his breath until he'd adjusted the stirrup. Then he dragged in air as he walked to Butch's right side.

"This is bothering you." Her low murmur added fuel to the flames.

"I'm okay."

"No, you're not. I can tell."

"It's being so close and wanting..." He huffed out a breath. "Never mind. You know."

"I do. I don't have an answer. These lessons are important."

"I won't have to adjust your stirrups next time."

"Why not?"

"Once I've got it right, I can adjust them to this length before you get here. I won't need to do it while you're on the horse."

"That'll help."

"Immensely." He sighed and stepped back. "Stand up again. I need to check the clearance between your crotch and the saddle."

"Good grief."

"Trust me, it's not supposed to be a sexual reference. Just do it."

She planted her feet and lifted her delectable tush. "How's the clearance?"

"Perfect. And so are you. Can't wait until Friday."

"Me, either."

"Thanks for that. It'll carry me through."

* * *

After Nell and Valerie left with the girls, Zeke braced himself for a barrage of questions and comments from his daughter. Never came.

Maybe during dinner? Nope. He'd talked to Henri about the riding demonstration in August and she'd okayed it, so Claire was eager to talk about that, plus her first barrel racing lesson with Auntie Ed, scheduled for the following morning. Claire had decided to call the Babes on Buckskins her aunties, to distinguish them from her aunts who lived on the ranch.

After dinner, they cleaned up the kitchen, played a few rounds of checkers and turned in early. She'd asked to shadow him during his work on the ranch, which meant she'd be up at dawn, same as him. They'd handle barn chores prior to heading over to Ed's at ten. She'd learned the term *shadowing* from Nell during the last week of school when the class had discussed their summer plans.

Following him around all summer had always been his daughter's summer plan and now she had a cool name for it. This week he'd teach her how to oil and repair tack. The Brotherhood was all over that idea. Most of them considered it boring.

Not Claire. "Can I start on the tack this afternoon, Dad?" She buckled herself into the passenger seat. She'd worn her Stetson for the trip to Ed's, but she held her riding helmet in her lap.

"The oiling, yes. I'll need to give you some instruction on repair techniques."

"How about tonight?"

"That works."

"I'm pretty good at sewing. Georgie's Spiderman costume keeps coming apart and I just sew it back together. The problem is he's too big for it, but he won't give it up."

"Because it makes him feel brave."

"That's why we let him keep wearing it. Aunt Anna bought him a new one, but he says it's not the same so he won't put it on."

"I get that. I can't imagine buying a new straw hat to replace this one."

She grinned. "Does your hat make you feel brave?"

He laughed. "Oh, definitely."

"Then it's lucky your head's not growing."

"Feels like it sometimes. Like it's gonna explode."

"Like yesterday whenever you looked at Miss O'Connor?"

Ah, there it was. He gave her a quick glance. She looked very pleased with herself. "Maybe."

"No maybe about it. Did you guys dance on Saturday night?"

"We did."

"*Yes.*" She punched a fist in the air. "I told my friends you must have. You were acting all goofy yesterday. I thought maybe you were coming down with something. Have you asked her out?"

"Um, yes, I have."

"Awesome! When's your date?"

"I'm taking her to the Moose on Friday night when the rest of the gang is going."

"Perfect." She settled into her seat with a smile.

He waited for more questions. None came. They drove in silence because he wasn't about to continue that thread if he didn't have to. But Claire's silence meant she was pondering something. It always did.

Whatever it was, she hadn't broached it by the time he turned onto the fancy paved drive leading to Ed's place. Edna Jane Vidal, eighty-five years young, had made good money as a barrel-racer and had invested wisely.

"Miss Jenson doesn't have a boyfriend." Claire's announcement seemed to come out of the blue, but he didn't believe that for a minute.

"How do you know that?" He drove slowly past the massive stone house and over to the warehouse-sized building that housed Ed's climate-controlled indoor riding arena.

"Piper asked her."

He smiled. Leave it to an eight-year-old to cut to the chase. "Maybe that's the way Miss Jenson likes it. Not everybody—"

"I know. But she wants a boyfriend. She told Piper she just hasn't found the right person."

"Then I hope she does. And I *also* hope you girls—"

"There's Uncle Teague!"

"Looks like he was waiting for us." As he parked the truck, Teague Sullivan, Ed's only wrangler these days, walked toward them.

Teague wasn't a member of the Brotherhood, and Claire had agonized over calling him Mr. Sullivan, which she said didn't feel right for someone she liked so much. Eventually, at Zeke's urging, she'd asked if she could call him Uncle Teague. He'd been delighted.

Claire unbuckled her seat belt and grabbed her helmet. "Which horse do you think I'll get? Do you think Uncle Teague's set up the barrels already?"

"Let's go find out."

An hour later, his fearless daughter was tired and covered in sawdust, but jubilant from the thrill of her first barrel-racing lesson. She sat on the bleachers at the end of the arena between him and Teague, with Ed perched on the seat below, turned around to face them.

"What a great start." Ed beamed at them. "Claire, you remind me of myself at your age. You have such a bright future in this sport."

"I *love* barrel-racing, Auntie Ed! I love it so much I can't stand it. I'm tired, but I'm not tired, if you know what I mean."

"I do."

"My outside is droopy but my inside is jumping around. And Cinnamon is the best horse ever."

"When I got him last year, I had no idea why I was doing it. I'd already found Toffee and his training was going well. I didn't need another horse, let alone a trained barrel racer. Turns out I needed him, after all."

"We appreciate the use of Cinnamon," Zeke said. "But that on top of free lessons feels like too much. I'd like to pay for—"

"Son, I would pay *you* for the privilege of teaching this girl. She's going to be phenomenal." She glanced at Claire. "But don't go getting a swelled head because I said that. Competitors who think too much of themselves usually go down in flames."

"I won't get a swelled head, Auntie Ed." She gave her auntie an impish smile. "Then my helmet won't fit."

Ed snorted. "All this and a sense of humor. We're going to have a great time this summer, Claire."

"We sure are. Oh, you know what? This summer my dad's teaching my friends to ride, plus Miss O'Connor and Miss Jenson. They're my teachers at school. And at the end of the lessons, we'll put on a demonstration. Gramma Henri said we could. You're definitely invited. You, too, Uncle Teague."

"Oh, I'll be there." Ed looked pleased at the prospect. "Thanks for inviting me."

"Sounds like fun, Zeke." Teague glanced at him over the top of Claire's head.

"It is. Those girls are a riot."

Teague grinned. "The big ones or the little ones?"

"He's talking about my friends," Claire said. "But Miss O'Connor and Miss Jenson are pretty funny, too. They kid each other a lot."

"I had a teacher named Miss Jenson when I was in school." Teague thumbed back his hat. "Loved her. My mom told me she's retired, now. I can't imagine that school without her."

"Well, *this* Miss Jenson isn't even *close* to retiring. She's around the same age as you and my dad. You'd like her."

Uh-oh. As Zeke scrambled for a way to block Claire's next move, she made an end run around him.

"Hey, I have an idea, Uncle Teague. If you have time, maybe you could come over and help my dad with the lessons."

"Claire, he's a busy guy. I doubt he—"

"Not *that* busy." He glanced at Ed. "You could spare me for an hour here and there, right?"

"Sure. No problem."

"And having Uncle Teague there would mean you could do more one-on-one teaching, Dad. And we'd learn faster."

Right. Claire's earnest tone might fool someone who didn't know her. They could miss the gleam of mischief in those innocent-looking blue eyes.

"I wouldn't want to get underfoot." But Teague looked eager for the opportunity. Not surprising since he loved any excuse to come over to the Buckskin. "But if I could be of some help..."

What the heck, maybe it wasn't such a bad idea. "Glad to have you."

16

Nell's emotions were all over the map as she parked beside the barn on Thursday. She was delighted to see Zeke, but the last lesson had given her a preview of how her excitement could escalate until it was embarrassingly obvious. She didn't want that.

"Looks like someone else is here." Val glanced at the flashy truck parked next to them. "Nice ride."

"Ooo, yeah." Riley peered out the window. "I love red trucks."

"It's pretty." Nell preferred Zeke's restored vintage one, but she wasn't going to say so in front of the girls. Claire was the ringleader of the matchmaking eight-year-olds, but the other three had become willing accomplices.

She and Val had been forced to issue an ultimatum during the ride home on Monday afternoon—her dating life and Val's lack of one were no longer appropriate topics of conversation. The girls had reluctantly agreed to the restriction.

"I'd think you'd rather talk about horses," Val had said, turning toward the back seat. "Isn't that why we're all doing this?"

"Mostly." Piper had appointed herself the spokesperson. "But I heard you say to Miss O'Connor that you wanted to get to know us better."

"Well, that's true. You'll be in my class next year, so getting to know each other will—"

"See? We're supposed to get to know *each other.*"

"To a point. Our dating life is beyond that point."

"Okay." Piper had let out a long-suffering sigh.

After that exchange, they'd seemed to comply, but their whispered conversations could have been about anything. More whispering had gone on today, too. On Monday night, while drinking the bottle of cab Val had won from Nell, they'd decided it was best to ignore the whispers.

As Nell exited the SUV and released the lock on the back doors so the girls could climb out, she glanced toward the barn. Prince, Lucky, Butch and Sundance stood by the hitching post, saddled and ready to go, but nobody was around.

Then Claire came out of the barn, waved and started toward them. "My Uncle Teague's here! He was showing me how to build a loop," she called out as she drew closer.

"A loop of what?" Tatum asked.

"Rope. Then you can twirl it around and rope something."

"I wanna learn that!"

"Who's Uncle Teague?" Piper walked faster. "I don't remember that name."

"Me, either." Riley clapped her hand to her head as a gust of wind threatened to blow off her hat. "I thought we met all your uncles on the field trip."

Zeke and a muscular cowboy Nell didn't recognize came through the open barn doorway and started in their direction.

"You didn't meet him because he doesn't live here," Claire said.

"That's a shame," Val said under her breath.

"Where's he from, then?" Tatum sounded impatient. "His truck has a Montana license plate."

Nell smiled. Tatum was fascinated with license plates. She couldn't see a vehicle without trying to identify the plate.

"I mean he doesn't live *here*." Claire swept an arm toward the barn and outbuildings. "On the ranch. He lives over at my Auntie Ed's place. He works for her."

Tatum put her hands on her hips. "How can he be your uncle, then?"

Claire looked uncertain, a flash of vulnerability in her expression. "Well... he said I could call him that."

"But if he doesn't—" Tatum ended her protest when Piper gave her a nudge and a look. "Um, okay."

Nell let out a breath. Her little speech to the girls in the car today had made an impression. They loved Claire. They also envied her for living on a ranch with so many horses and a host of adopted aunts and uncles. In their eyes, she had it all. Nell had pointed out that Claire didn't have what all three of them had—a devoted mother.

They'd taken that to heart at the time. But adding yet another uncle had clearly pushed Tatum's buttons. And speaking of pushing buttons...

Zeke came toward her with that special glow in his dark eyes. Her body warmed and her heart pounded. *Tomorrow night.*

"Ladies." Zeke's gaze shifted to encompass everyone. "I'd like you to meet a good friend and a top-notch wrangler, Teague Sullivan. He's offered to help with the lessons."

Nell caught Valerie's soft hum of approval and swallowed a laugh. Had Claire had anything to do with this? Wouldn't be a stretch.

Zeke introduced each of them to Teague and Val made a point of shaking his hand, even though she had to reach over Tatum to do it.

Tatum swung her arms back and forth. "Mr. Sullivan, can you teach us to build a loop?"

"I will if there's time."

"Woo-hoo!" Tatum executed a short victory dance.

"We'd better get started then." Zeke motioned them toward the barn. Now he had a rival for those girls' attention.

Tatum's irritation at being presented with yet another doting uncle had vanished by the time she'd traded her hat for a helmet. When she was ready to mount Prince, she asked Teague to help her up.

Piper, though, remained loyal to Zeke, stepping into his cupped hands to mount Lucky.

Once she was in the saddle, Zeke turned to address the group. "Since Teague's offered his assistance for these lessons, we've decided to shake things up a bit. We tacked up the horses, but at the end of the lesson, we'll have a hands-on session on removing the tack and grooming the horses. Next Monday, you'll learn how to tack them up yourself."

"Yay!" Tatum glanced over at Piper. "Aren't you excited?"

"I am, but these saddles look heavy and the horses are tall."

"All true, Piper," Teague said. "So we'll give you techniques to deal with those issues."

Val leaned close to Nell. "I love a man with techniques."

"I think Claire's counting on it."

"She did this?"

"He works for the lady who's giving her barrel racing lessons."

"Oh. I didn't put that together. What a little devil."

"Are you upset?"

Val chuckled. "Not exactly."

"Didn't think so. Let's go mount up." She glanced at Val. "Unless you want that broad-shouldered cowboy to assist you?"

"Heck, no. If he's drawn to the helpless female type, then he's not for me. Let's get this show on the road." She buckled her helmet, marched over to Sundance and swung into the saddle as if she'd been doing it all her life.

Nell envied Val her long legs. She approached Butch with the same show of confidence, but her mounting technique had a herky-jerky quality. Although she made it into the saddle, it wasn't pretty. She cussed a little under her breath.

"Something wrong?" Zeke's soft question caught her by surprise. He stood beside her, hat pushed back, head tilted so he could meet her gaze.

Her heart did a stutter-step. "I wish I could get on and off more gracefully. I know I need the stirrups to be adjusted like that because my legs are shorter than Val's, but it's harder for me to reach the stirrup with my foot. And after I do, I'm off-balance."

He nodded. "Which means you might have to start doing push-ups."

"Why? I'm just holding the reins."

"That's after you use your strong arms to pull yourself into the saddle."

"Oh. Pushups, huh?"

"It's a simple way to build up strength in your arms and upper body."

"I suppose it is, but I'm a dunce when it comes to working out. I aced all my high school classes except gym. I nearly flunked gym. How sad is that?"

"Tell you what. I'll give you some pointers tomorrow night."

She stared at him, her heart racing. "Wh-what?"

His gaze was steady, but laughter gleamed in the depths of those dark eyes. "Perfect opportunity, right?"

"I can't believe you said that. Now I'm thinking about—"

"Exactly what I've been thinking about for three solid days. Welcome to the club."

_17_

"You look great in that black shirt, Dad. Are you excited about your date?"

"Sure am." It took all he had to make that response sound casual. He put the truck in gear and pulled away from the bunkhouse. "Are you excited to be spending the night at Gramma Henri's?"

"I can't wait! We're going to have so much fun. Those trains in the basement are awesome, Dad. I can't believe you and my uncles haven't been down there yet. Georgie loves them, too."

"We keep talking about it. To tell the truth, I think some of your uncles are afraid they'll get emotional."

"That's what Gramma Henri said. She was at first, but she got over it. She said Charley would want someone to enjoy them."

"I'll bring it up with Jake. He'll give me the straight scoop." He loved being able to count on that.

"I have my fingers crossed for Uncle Teague and Miss Jenson. I hope they have a good time."

"They probably will." He had to admit Val and Teague had gravitated to each other from the get-go. Val had already planned to go to the Moose with the Buckskin gang. Teague's offer to pick her up on his way into town made perfect sense. But none of that would have happened without Claire.

"I had a feeling they'd like each other. Wish I could be there to see how it goes. I don't suppose you would—"

"Spy on them?"

"Not spy, exactly. I'd just like to know—"

"Sorry, sweetie. I won't give you a report on their date." *Or mine.*

"I knew you'd say that." She sighed. "I get it. Whatever happens is their private business."

"Exactly."

"Don't worry. I won't ask you to report on your date with Miss O'Connor, either."

"Good."

"I don't need a report, anyway. I know you'll both have an amazing time. I—oh, look! There's Uncle Garrett and Aunt Anna with Georgie. We arrived when they did. Hey, they could leave their truck here and ride into town with you!"

"Well, actually—"

"No, you're right. Bad idea. I don't know what I was thinking."

His breath caught. Was she aware he'd be spending the night at Nell's? If she was, that made him a little uncomfortable. She was eight, so she probably had some knowledge about what went on between couples.

But he hadn't ever discussed the birds and the bees with her. He'd figured on waiting until she was... nine? Hell, he had no idea when it would be appropriate. He needed some advice on that before long. In fact, he should—

"You can't all ride in your truck, Dad. Your backseat's way too small."

"You're so right, sweetie." He shut off the engine and breathed a sigh of relief. *The talk* could wait a while longer.

No sooner was Claire out of the truck, her overnight bag in her hand, than she was assaulted by Georgie. He grabbed her free hand and tugged her toward the porch steps. "Sissy! Come on! We play trains!"

Anna laughed and glanced over at Zeke. "You'd think they hadn't seen each other in months."

"To Georgie, last Sunday probably feels like months." Zeke lowered his voice as he drew closer to Garrett. "Appreciate you taking Claire for the day on Sunday. I was..." He trailed off and managed a sheepish grin. "Not quite with the program."

"Glad to do it." Garrett squeezed his shoulder. "She's a big help to us."

"That's for sure," Anna said. "I love having her around and Georgie *really* loves it."

"Claire does, too. She talks about him all the time. He's the little brother she always wanted."

"I see that." Garrett smiled as he watched Claire slowly climb the steps so Georgie could keep up with her. "We'd offer to repeat the situation tomorrow, but I'm escorting a large group on a trail ride and Anna's taking Georgie to day care. Jake desperately needs her at Raptors Rise. They're crazy busy."

"That's good to hear, and I would never assume you'd cover for me every weekend. I'll be in better shape tomorrow. I'll make sure of it. Clare's supposed to be shadowing me this summer, so I'll be introducing her to the joys of digging post holes."

"Funny thing is, for her it will be a joy. I've never seen a kid so exciting about ranch chores as that girl."

Zeke nodded. "This is her happy place, all right." He glanced at his phone. "I need to get going, but first I'm going to pop in and tell Claire goodbye."

"We're right behind you. I'm not sure Georgie cares whether we say goodbye. He's usually too involved in whatever he and Claire are doing. The goodbye part is more for Anna and me."

"Right. We want them to be self-sufficient, but..."

"We still hope they need us," Anna said. "At least a little bit."

Henri had the kids in the living room taking pictures of them in the engineer's hats she'd bought them.

"Oh, my goodness!" Anna grabbed her phone and hurried to do the same. "Henri, you realize you're spoiling these children."

"That's a gramma's privilege." She picked up a baby version of the hat. "This one's for Cleo Marie. She won't be here for another fifteen minutes or so. When I get one of all three of them, I'll send them to you."

"Great."

The goodbye scene was short and sweet, because Claire and Georgie were impatient to head for the basement. Zeke thanked Henri for the hat and her willingness to keep his daughter overnight.

"I have more fun than they do," Henri said with a smile.

"I just want you to know how much I appreciate—"

"I know you do, Zeke. You're a good man and a wonderful dad. Now go have a great time with Nell. You deserve some fun, too."

"Thank you, ma'am." He put on his hat, touched two fingers to the brim, and left. He was running a few minutes behind, so he swung into the driver's seat and sent a short text to Nell. *Leaving Henri's now. Be there as soon as I can.*

Her reply came zipping back. *I'll be waiting. Don't speed.*

He'd planned to do exactly that and keep an eye out for cops. *Okay, I won't.* So now he couldn't. And the limit was fifty-five.

He kept the needle on the double nickel and tapped the steering wheel, his nerves screaming at him to push the pedal to the metal. Other vehicles passed him, which was humiliating but bearable because he didn't know them. Then CJ swerved around him while honking and waving out the window. Cheeky bastard. To be fair, though, hardly anyone did fifty-five on this road, especially when it was still light out.

After an eternity, he arrived at her bungalow as sunset bathed the house in golden light. Parking quickly, he jumped out and hurried up the walk, the blood pumping through his veins as he took the porch steps two at a time.

She pushed open the screen door. "Hi. I'm glad you wore that black shirt."

"You said you liked it." He stepped inside and reached for her. Then he paused and gazed at her carefully applied makeup. It was much more elaborate than she'd worn last week and included sparkles on her eyelids and something that made her red lips gleam like satin. "If I do what I intended to do, I'll mess you up."

"I could repair it."

"No, that wouldn't be right. You look beautiful, Nell. Not more beautiful than you are without it, but I'll bet you had fun putting it on."

"I did. The fancy stuff matches my mood. Tonight, I'm not Miss O'Connor, circumspect grade-school teacher."

"Oh?" He smiled. "Who might you be, then?"

She stroked a hand up his chest. "I'm Eleanor, sex goddess, worshipped by handsome cowboys like yourself."

He swallowed. "You've got that right. And if we don't head out to my truck immediately, I'll start worshipping ASAP."

"Then let's go." She grabbed the same small purse she'd had a week ago, picked up her keys lying next to it, and started out the door. "We promised each other we'd go to the Moose tonight and hang out with the Buckskin gang."

"Yes, ma'am." He followed her out and waited while she locked the door. "But I didn't know I'd be dealing with Eleanor, sex goddess."

She laughed. "Neither did I, but I went shopping today and bought a few things."

"Like that outfit?" He'd been so focused on not kissing her that he hadn't paid attention to what she had on. He stepped back to admire the combo of a low-cut white knit tank top and a swirly white skirt, both decorated with silver beads. "I like it."

"It kinda goes with your black shirt. A yin/yang thing."

"That round symbol with the black and white parts curved against each other?"

"Yes, that."

"That always seemed sexual to me."

"It is, in a way." She tucked her keys in her purse and started across the porch. "I bought party boots, too."

"Sexy." The short white boots also had silver bling. The memory of stroking her shapely calves made his fingers curl.

"The party boots suit Eleanor. Everything does, including my undies."

He sucked in a breath. "You really shouldn't have told me that."

"Oh, but I had to. That's how a sex goddess operates. She teases you with the possibilities and then makes you wait for it until you're crazy with lust."

"What if the crazy-with-lust part has already happened?"

She glanced over her shoulder and flashed him a grin. "Then you're in for a challenging evening."

He groaned.

"Don't feel too bad. It'll be challenging for me, too. My lacy white panties are already damp."

Her shenanigans might be the death of him, but he'd die a happy man.

18

Nell had never made a grand entrance in her life. But walking into the Choosy Moose on the arm of Zeke Lassiter while wearing a sexy outfit qualified. Maybe everyone in the room didn't turn and stare, but many did.

"Hey, look at you, girlfriend." Val came over from the bar, a drink in her hand and Teague right behind her. "Look at *both* of you. Did you coordinate your outfits?"

Nell laughed and shook her head. "Not exactly. I knew Zeke had a fancy black shirt with silver piping and I bought my outfit thinking it would be a fun matchup if he showed up in the shirt. And he did."

Teague grinned. "I hope you've been practicing your dance moves. Folks are gonna expect a performance."

"I didn't think of that." Nell grimaced. "You mean like *Dancing with the Stars*? I wasn't trying to—"

"Nah, I'm just teasing you. You both look terrific. Come on over. We saved you a place."

"In the booth?"

"The booth was maxed out when we arrived. They tried to squeeze us in, but since I knew you two were coming, I grabbed us a four-top right next to the booth. Sitting at a table will give us easier access to the dance floor."

"Good idea, Teague. Thanks."

"It's a great idea," Nell said. "I just want to take a minute to say hello to everybody."

"I'll go with you."

Nell stepped over to the booth, Zeke by her side, his arm around her waist. Judging from all those smiling faces, the gang approved the matchup. "Hey, everybody."

"Hey, yourself," Isabel said. "Nice outfit!"

"Thanks. How's Cleo Marie's teething situation?"

"Better, thank goodness. You have to see this shot of her with Claire and Georgie. Henri gave them all train engineer's hats." She pulled out her phone and tapped on it before handing it across the table.

"Oh, my gosh." In a large easy chair, Claire held the baby on her lap and Georgie snuggled next to her. They each wore a gray-and-white striped cap. "I love it. Look, Zeke."

"Very cute. I'll bet I have one on my phone. Henri said she'd text one to me once Cleo Marie was there."

"Which reminds me," CJ's eyes gleamed with mischief. "Why were you poking along the road into town like you were out for a Sunday drive?"

"I… um… promised Nell I wouldn't speed."

Her breath caught. Clearly he'd taken her request *very* seriously. She slipped her arm around his waist and gave a little squeeze as she murmured a quick *thank you.*

"Dude, nobody does fifty-five on that road. It's—"

"He was keeping his promise to his lady," Jake said, warmth in his voice. "My brother and I are big on keeping our promises, right, Zeke?

"Yes, sir."

"Come to think of it," Matt said, "So was Charley."

"That he was." CJ lifted his cider bottle in Zeke's direction. "I stand corrected. Well done, Zeke."

Jake lifted his bottle, too. "Here's to you, little brother. I imagine you're thirsty after that long, slow drive. I recommend you and your lady snag yourselves a cool one."

"Will do." His hand tightened on her waist as he started to turn around.

"See you all on the dance floor," she called over her shoulder. Then she leaned closer to Zeke. "That was very sweet. I had no idea you'd take me that literally."

"Couldn't see a way around it. Anything over fifty-five is technically speeding."

She glanced up at him. "I have the urge to kiss you right now."

He smiled. "Nice to know. Hold that thought."

Their table was only steps away. When they reached it, he pulled out her chair and helped her into it. That's when the reality hit her.

She was on a date with Zeke Lassiter. He was hers for the evening—for dinner and for dancing. And for... her whole body flushed with anticipation.

"Nell?" He touched her hand where it rested on the table. "You okay?"

She met his gaze. "I've never been better."

"Glad to hear it. When you didn't answer me, I got worried."

"What did you say?"

"I asked what you'd like to drink. The wait staff looks busy, so I'll go to the bar and fetch it."

She glanced at Teague and Val, who each had a glass of what looked like champagne. An ice bucket sat on the far side of the table "Is that what I think it is?"

Teague lifted his glass. "We felt like celebrating. If you'd like some, I'll get us a couple more glasses and order a second bottle."

She hesitated. It might be more expensive than regular wine. Probably was.

Before she'd made a choice. Zeke spoke up. "Is that the kind Ed likes?"

"Yes."

"Then let's go with it. If you like champagne at all, Nell, you'll love this one."

"I do like it, but—"

"Then it's decided. Teague, I'll head over to the bar with you."

"Alrighty." Teague pushed back his chair. "Ladies, if you'll excuse us."

"Of course." Valerie winked at him. "Gives us a chance to talk about you while you're gone."

Teague's eyebrows lifted. "Women do that, too?"

"Smart-aleck."

"Hey, it cuts both ways. Come on, Zeke. Let's go talk about the ladies."

"My favorite topic." He touched two fingers to the brim of his hat.

After they left, Nell gestured to Val's glass. "is that pricey?"

"I think it might be. It's the best I've ever tasted, that's for sure. Teague suggested getting a bottle and I love champagne, so I went along with it."

"I don't want this date to cost Zeke an arm and a leg."

"If you want my opinion, I think he knows exactly what he's getting into and is thrilled to do something special for you. Just like you bought a new outfit to look special for him."

"I was inspired to go shopping."

"Good. He's a sweetie."

"You have no idea. Did you hear the comments over there about his driving?"

"Sorry. I was absorbed in staring into Teague's beautiful eyes. What did I miss?"

Nell filled her in.

"Sounds like you found yourself an honorable man."

"Sure does. You seem very happy with Teague, too."

"I like him a lot. He makes me laugh. Right off the bat he told me about his first love, an elementary teacher coincidentally named Miss Jenson."

"That's supposed to be funny? Bringing up a former—"

"He was six at the time."

"Oh." She grinned. "Okay, that's funny."

"And touching. He estimates now that she was probably in her thirties. She was the most beautiful woman he'd ever seen except in the movies. He told her he'd marry her as soon as he grew up."

"Adorable."

"Especially the way he tells it. Have you noticed his dimples?"

"No, but it's an excellent sign that you have."

"That's not all I've noticed. Can't wait to find out if the guy has rhythm."

"On the dance floor."

"Yes, that, but..." Val leaned closer. "You know what they say. Dancing is foreplay with your clothes on."

She lifted her eyebrows. "You're already considering—"

"I know, I know." She lowered her voice. "But the chemistry's there, and..." She glanced toward the bar. "Here they come." She straightened and picked up her champagne flute. "So I told him about the time a student proposed to me."

"When was this?"

"A couple of years ago. Billy Harvey. He avoided me in the halls this year. I think he remembers, and now that's he's a mature eleven, he's embarrassed." She looked up as Teague arrived followed by Zeke. "Mission accomplished?"

"We have glasses and a second bottle is on the way."

"I'm telling her about Billy Harvey."

Teague smiled. "Your nine-year-old admirer."

"One of your students had a crush on you?" Zeke set down both glasses and Teague filled them from the bottle sitting in the ice bucket.

"Yes, poor kid."

"It never occurred to me that might happen," Nell said. "How did you handle it?"

"I told him I was honored that he'd asked. But unfortunately, I had someone special in my life who would be upset if I accepted his proposal."

"Did you have someone special?"

"My dad."

Nell cracked up. "Good one."

"Hey, it wasn't a lie! Guaranteed he'd be upset if his daughter agreed to marry a nine-year-old."

Nell looked over at Teague. "What did your Miss Jenson say when you proposed?"

His dimples flashed. "That I was very handsome, but she was looking for someone slightly older."

"Aw. That's good, too, but I'm gonna use Val's line if the subject ever comes up."

"You're welcome to it, girlfriend. Just make sure you don't laugh. Don't even chuckle."

"Val's right. I was only six, but I was deadly serious. I would have been devastated if she'd laughed at me."

A server arrived with the second bottle of champagne, uncorked it and tucked it in the ice bucket along with the first one. "Are you folks ready to order or should I come back?"

"We need a minute," Teague said.

"Take your time. Give me a signal when you're ready." He tipped his hat and left.

Teague grinned. "I should come here with teachers more often. Best service ever."

"All I know is that the service was wonderful during the party Ben threw for the teachers."

"And that kid was assigned to us that night," Val said. He probably remembers Nell and me were there and knows Ben wants teachers to be treated with TLC."

Teague laughed. "Either that, or you have another proposal coming."

"I'll just tell him I'm taken."

"By all means." Teague picked up his menu. "Guess we'd better decide."

Nell opened her menu and chose a medium-priced meal. Despite what Val said about Zeke wanting to treat her like a queen, she wasn't about to add an expensive meal to his tab.

He glanced around the table. "Everybody ready?" When they all nodded, he turned toward the bar and started to lift his hand. Then he lowered it again. "He was watching for it. Teague, I'm with you. We need to bring teachers with us from now on."

"Works for me." Nell sipped from her flute. Whoa. Good stuff.

While they gave their order, she took another swallow. *Very* nice.

After he left, Val lifted her glass. "We need a toast. Here's to a memorable night."

Teague picked up his. "I'll drink to that."

"I'll absolutely drink to that." Zeke winked at Nell before raising his glass.

All four met with a soft click in the center of the table. As Nell put the glass to her lips, she met Zeke's dark gaze. Slowly his attention lowered to her mouth. Her breath caught. How long before they could make their excuses and leave?

Not until after dinner, for sure. And they should dance a few times. She tipped the glass and drank. They wouldn't be going out the door any time soon.

She'd best calm the heck down and shift her attention away from the sexy cowboy to her left. Taking another swallow, she gave Teague a smile. "This champagne tastes great. You said this was the kind your boss likes?"

"Yes, ma'am."

"What is it?"

"Cristal."

"Never heard of it. But I like it."

Zeke reached for the bottle nestled in the ice bucket. "Then let me top off your glass."

"By all means." She held it out. "I'm ready to party."

_19_

Zeke had pulled out all the stops to convince Teague to share the cost of that expensive bubbly. This was his first date in years, damn it, and he wasn't letting some other man buy his lady's champagne.

He'd forgotten the thrill of treating a woman to a night of dinner and dancing. Nell brought out romantic impulses that he'd kept buried for some time. Yvette's barrage of insults and putdowns had staunched the tender feelings he'd once had for her.

After she admitted cheating on him, his only goal had been protecting Claire, being the solid, dependable parent she desperately needed. His own sexuality had become irrelevant, a nuisance, in fact, to be contained as best he could.

Until Nell. Until their explosive encounter a week ago. And now, flirting with her over dinner and holding her in his arms on the dance floor reawakened an instinct to be there for her, the man she turned to, her hero.

But he wasn't that single guy with no responsibilities he'd been ten years ago. He'd do well to keep that in mind, enjoy the moment and keep a tight rein on his tendency to dream.

They'd just finished an energetic two-step and he'd pulled her in tight for the finish when she glanced up at him, her breathing as erratic as his. "How soon can we leave?"

He gulped as the implications of that questions set fire to his privates. "Whenever you want."

"I think..." She paused to take a breath. "I think we can go after one more dance. Then we can vamoose."

"Fine with me." More than fine. He'd been keeping the heat down to a simmer because dragging her out of there right after dessert wouldn't have been the gentlemanly thing to do. Instead he'd waited for her to decide. She just had.

She gazed up at him. "Whaddya know? It's my favorite song."

"*Amarillo by Morning* is your favorite song?"

Snuggling against him, she gazed into his eyes. "It is tonight."

* * *

Finally. Nell was tucked into the passenger seat of Zeke's truck and he'd switched on the engine. They'd bid everyone goodbye and suffered through the sly grins and knowing winks. It went with the territory and he didn't mind. He didn't mind anything at this moment. Nell's bungalow was only minutes away.

He put the truck in reverse and paused. "Any instructions?"

"About what?"

"How you want me to drive to your house?"

Her laughter was soft, enticing. "I trust you won't do eighty through the streets of Apple Grove."

"No, ma'am. Might feel like it, but I won't." He checked for traffic, non-existent this time on a Friday night, and backed out. "You have to watch on summer nights. Could be a raccoon or a skunk crossing the road."

"Good to know." She glanced over at him. "I was touched that you kept your speed at fifty-five all the way into town tonight."

"Wasn't easy."

"But you're a stickler for keeping your word?"

"Yes, ma'am."

"It's an admirable trait. Clearly it's important to the Brotherhood, too."

"It is, and I appreciate that."

"I could be wrong, but..." She hesitated. "Jake's comment made it sound like truthfulness has extra significance for you two."

Not surprising she'd lock onto Jake's statement. His big brother had been focused on supporting him. He loved Jake for stepping up like that. But Nell was like Claire, sensitive to the undercurrents.

He didn't want to discuss his dad tonight. His father's shameful behavior sickened him. And he'd have to make Nell promise to keep it to herself.

The Buckskin gang knew everything since he and Jake had both been affected by it. But Claire was still oblivious, and they'd all agreed to keep it that way.

"You don't want to talk about it."

He glanced at her. "Not now."

"Okay."

The mood change was subtle. A little of the warmth was gone from her voice. He didn't like it. "It's not a pretty story."

"I get it, Zeke. I didn't mean to pry into your private business."

"You don't have to apologize. You pick up on things. Nothing wrong with that. I'd just rather not go into it, at least not now, when we're—"

"Seriously, it's fine." She reached over and squeezed his arm. "I like you. A lot. And I gather you've been put through the grinder. Sometimes it helps to talk about it and I'm a very good listener. But clearly this isn't the right time."

The tightness in his chest loosened. "Thank you."

"For what?"

"For not pushing. For not getting upset because I won't... I don't know... open up." He parked in front of her bungalow, switched off the engine and unbuckled his seat belt. He turned to her. "You're a good friend, Nell."

She smiled as she unfastened her seatbelt, too. "Don't forget I'm a friend with benefits."

He reached across the console and cupped her face in both hands. "There's zero chance I'll forget that." Leaning toward her, he nibbled at her mouth. "You taste delicious." He ran his tongue over her bottom lip. "Is that stuff you put on flavored?"

"Mm-hm." She slid her hand behind his head and pulled him closer. "Cherry."

"I like it." He outlined her top lip with the tip of his tongue.

"Then you'll like the body oil, too."

He drew back, a surge of lust stealing his breath. "Body oil?"

"It's on my bedside table."

He let go of her and reached for the door handle. "Then time's a-wastin', pretty lady."

20

Nell quivered in anticipation as a magnificently naked Zeke straddled her hips and unscrewed the cap from a small bottle of cherry-flavored oil.

Pressing his finger to the top of the bottle, he tipped it over, righted it again and tasted the oil on his finger. "That'll do."

"Glad you..." She cleared the huskiness from her throat. "Glad you like it."

"I like this whole program." His hot gaze swept over her bare breasts. "Done this before, have you?"

"Never."

His dark eyebrows arched. "But you had everything ready, right down to the beach towel spread over the sheet."

"In case you get a little wild with the oil."

"I intend to get very wild with the oil. Starting now." He dribbled it in a circle on her left breast.

She gasped at the cool liquid touched her warm skin.

"Oh, look at that. It's starting to drip. Can't have that." He set the bottle on the nightstand and cupped her breast. "Playtime." Leaning over her, he began the slow process of driving her out of her mind.

By the time he'd worked his way down to her hips, the combo of fragrant oil and his talented mouth had destroyed her inhibitions. She opened her thighs in a blatant invitation.

His low chuckle was the sexiest sound in the world. "Are you trying to tell me something?"

"Yes."

"Say it."

She gulped. Maybe not *all* her inhibitions were gone.

The bottle in one hand, he slid up her slick body and made love to her mouth, thrusting his tongue deep, kissing her with abandon, stoking the flames. Then he lifted his head. "Say it," he murmured, his gaze locked with hers. "Tell me what you want."

And she did, using words she'd never spoken to a man, words that tightened her core and quickened his breathing.

His eyes turned almost black and his voice was thick with desire. "My pleasure."

Easing back down, he tipped the bottle, using generous amounts of the fragrant oil as he stroked and massaged her aching pleasure center. Then he laid the empty bottle on the towel, pushed his hands under her hips and dipped his head.

When his mouth made contact, she cried out. And the cries kept coming as he settled in and took her to heights unknown until... *Zeke. Zeke. Zeke....* She called his name until she was hoarse. The powerful waves of her climax left her gasping and shaking. He held her, his big hands steady, his murmured words coaxing her back to shore.

Slowly he lowered her hips and planted soft kisses along her inner thigh as he moved off the bed. The empty bottle landed on the nightstand with a soft click. Foil ripped and latex snapped. Then he was back, rising over her, seeking entrance, gliding his firm cock into her trembling channel.

Wrapping her arms around his muscular back, she lifted her gaze, certain she'd find desperation in his eyes, intense passion fueled by days of waiting, a jaw tight with the effort to restrain himself.

But no. Instead... tenderness. Her heart stalled. Caring, tenderness and... something more. Something life-changing. Did he know?

Maybe not.

She tightened her grip. "Make love to me."

"Yes, ma'am." He began to move, but the crazy, untethered sexual adventure they'd shared a week ago had become richer. Every breath, every soft murmur resonated with new meaning.

The light that flared in his eyes as he pushed deep hadn't been there before. He was taking his time, savoring the connection.

And so was she. Every gentle stroke, every precious moment of intimacy—such treasures. She reveled in the sweet friction. Gloried in the subtle rise of tension.

His movements were fluid, relaxed... *joyful*. The gradual increase in pace flowed naturally. His gaze never left hers.

Her core muscles tightened and his mouth curved in a slow smile. "There you go."

That knowing smile sent liquid heat rushing to greet his next thrust. "Are you... close?"

"Yes." His breathing had roughened, but not by much. "When you come, I'll come."

Dragging in more air, she moved her hands lower, cupping his glutes, pushing her fingertips into the rippling muscles. "Good."

The light in his eyes brightened. "Sure is." He bore down a bit more. And more yet.

Another thrust and she'd be... *there*. She arched her back. "Now!"

"Ah, Nell." With a low groan, he drove home and shuddered, gasping her name as the pulses of his climax blended with the rolling rhythm of hers.

Glorious.

As the aftershocks lessened, he rested his forehead on her shoulder and gulped for air. She stroked his damp hair, yearning to prolong the wonder of what they'd just experienced. They'd transcended bodily pleasure to create lovemaking that was... irresistible. She wanted more of it.

At last he stirred, lifted his head and gazed down at her. He opened his mouth as if to say something, closed it again and shook his head. "I don't... that was..."

"Special."

He nodded. "Yes." He took a shaky breath. "I'm getting up. Do you want anything?"

"Just you."

"I'll be right back."

She watched him leave, marveling at the beauty of his broad shoulders, narrow hips and strong thighs. She was a lucky woman.

He wasn't gone long, and when he returned, he carried a damp washcloth. "I thought you might feel a little sticky."

"I do." She grinned. "I can't for the life of me figure out why."

"It's a mystery." He lifted the washcloth. "May I?"

"Sounds like fun."

"I'm not trying to seduce you." Sitting on the edge of the bed, he carefully wiped her breasts.

"Are you sure?"

"No. But full disclosure, I'm a normal guy with normal recovery time. So even if I get you hot, I won't be party ready yet."

"No worries. After that last go-round, I doubt I'm seduce-able."

He chuckled. "Is that a challenge?" He ran the washcloth over her stomach.

"It's a fact. That was a primo experience. I want to bask in it for a while."

"Me, too." He continued to move the warm cloth over her sensitized skin. "I have something I'd—" He paused. "Maybe you should finish up." He stood and swept a hand toward his crotch. "A mind of its own."

"Wow. I'm flattered." She scooted to a sitting position and took the washcloth from his outstretched hand.

"You get to me, Nell."

"Ditto, Zeke." She smiled. "You might want to turn your head."

"Good advice." He looked away while she finished the job.

"Thank you. I'm done."

He glanced at her, his gaze warm as he took the washcloth. "I really do want some cuddle time. I'll take this back and have a talk with my friend."

"Would you please take this, too?" She rolled away from the towel and picked it up.

He reached for it. "See you soon." When he returned, his *friend* no longer stood at attention. "This is a wonderful bed." He climbed in and gathered her into his arms.

"Yeah, well, you sleep in a bunk."

"And I'm fine with that. It's the best option for now. Your bed is nicer, though, especially with you in it."

"You're welcome anytime."

"I know. Wish it could be more often." He drew her close and cradled her head against his shoulder. "That business we talked about in the truck—"

"You don't have to tell me."

"I do, though. Whatever this is between us—it's important."

"Yes."

"We're important to each other. And to Claire. What I'm about to tell you—she doesn't know and doesn't need to know. Not now, anyway. Someday she'll find out, but I want to postpone that moment. She's already had to deal with a mother who..."

"Wasn't ideal."

"That's a nice way of putting it." He rested his cheek on the top of her head and tucked her even more securely into the curve of his body. "My father—and Jake's—is a bigamist."

"That still happens?" It didn't sound real to her.

"Unfortunately."

"But we have databases, now. Everyone keeps records. How does he get away with it?"

"I don't know. Don't really care. But he's somehow convinced two different women that he's their lawfully wedded husband—Jake's mom and mine." His body had become increasingly tense.

She rubbed his back, attempting to soothe his agitation. "When did you find out?"

"When I compared notes with Jake. My dad told me I had a half-brother and he led me to believe Jake was the result of a former love affair, one he'd broken off when he met my mom. That's what Claire still believes."

"But he had to know you'd figure out the truth when you came to Montana and talked to Jake."

"I'm guessing he's counting on my loyalty not to turn him in. Maybe even Jake's loyalty, although I can tell you Jake has no interest in protecting him."

"A man like that doesn't deserve loyalty. How does he live with himself?"

"You'd have to ask him."

"And how does he physically manage the logistics? That can't be a simple matter."

"I'm sure it's not. He travels for business, which gives him plenty of leeway. He and my mom have been married for thirty-two years and she's... she's very trusting."

"But since Jake's the reason you guys moved here, your dad must have told your mom that much, at least."

"Not after he swore me and Claire to secrecy. He convinced us the shock would be too much for her."

"My God. What an operator. How did he explain your move?"

"He told her he'd heard about the place during a recent business trip and knew it would be perfect for Claire and me since we've always wanted to live on a ranch."

"What about Jake's mom? Does she know about you?"

"She doesn't, but Jake says she wouldn't be surprised that my dad fathered a kid with another woman. He repeatedly divorced and remarried Jake's mother. I guess there were periods when he wasn't a bigamist, but he just remarried Jake's mom, so it's true for now."

"I'm sorry, Zeke." She hugged him. "You must hate this."

"Oh, yeah, I do."

"Have you thought of turning him in?"

"Constantly. Now that Jake knows, he has the same thoughts. But we'd ruin our mothers' lives in the process."

"Ruin them? You'd free them from a toxic man!"

"Would they thank us? I'm not sure they would. The most innocent victim would be Claire. I doubt we could expose him and keep her in the dark. The truth could send her into a tailspin. She loves her Grampa Bud. And she's a romantic. If she found out how he's treated her Gramma Frannie...."

Nell took a shaky breath. "What a mess."

"Yes, ma'am."

"I'm glad you told me." Her heart ached for him. First his wife, then his dad. He'd been knocked six ways to Sunday. No wonder he wanted to hang onto the status quo. "Even more than that, thank you for trusting me with the information."

"You can't even tell Val."

"I won't. Is Claire close to her grandparents, then? Does she miss them?"

"I'm afraid so."

"Now that you mention it, she told me something about a playhouse they'd built for her in their backyard."

"They did that last year, when Claire and I were living in an apartment. It was their way of giving her something special. My dad and I built it and my mom and Claire painted, furnished and decorated it."

"Are they in touch?"

"They call my cell and I let Claire do most of the talking. My mom wanted us to come back for a visit after school let out. I told her I was a new hire and couldn't leave for that long. And my dad's throwing up roadblocks to keep them from coming here."

"Poor Claire. Poor you. I wish there was something I could do."

Putting a finger under her chin, he tilted her face up. "There is." He brushed his mouth against hers. "And you're doing it."

_21_

Once again, Zeke found comfort in Nell's arms. And so much pleasure. She was a bountiful feast, one he appreciated far more this time than the first night they'd spent together. He learned to sip and taste instead of gobbling voraciously.

She also taught him to play. The flavored oil had been a start. Then she reminded him about the pushups he'd teased her about. Coaching her in that exercise started with laughter and ended with a steamy episode featuring Nell taking the top position and driving him insane.

And finally, she offered the radical suggestion of getting some rest. Holding her close, he drifted into a deeper sleep than he'd had in many months, maybe even years. Good thing he'd set his phone alarm.

Silencing the soft chime quickly, he slipped out of bed and headed for the shower. The bungalow's fixtures and plumbing were old and cranky. They groaned in protest when he turned on the water.

He winced at making so much noise. Couldn't be helped. He needed to be fresh as a daisy when he picked up Claire at Henri's. Maybe Nell was a sound sleeper.

But as he dried off, he smelled coffee. Not such a sound sleeper. Dressing quickly, he breathed in the scent of raisin-bread toast. When he walked into the kitchen, she turned from the counter where she was spreading peanut butter on the toast. "I hope you have ten minutes."

"I do." He'd rather spend it kissing her than eating toast and drinking coffee, but kissing Nell when she was wearing nothing but a fluffy bathrobe would be a recipe for... well, not disaster. Extreme lateness, though.

She handed him a mug of coffee and a small plate with the toast cut in four triangles.

"Thanks. Nice presentation."

She laughed as she picked up her coffee and toast. "Kids like their sandwiches cut that way and I just automatically do it, now."

"No worries. I'm just a big kid at heart." He set his plate and mug on the kitchen table so he could pull out a chair for her.

"If you dig deep enough, most of us are still kids underneath. That's why I can relate to my third graders. My eight-year-old is alive and well in my grown-up body."

"I know." He settled into his chair, dug his phone from his pocket and laid it by his plate so he'd keep track of the time. "I couldn't say who was more excited about that greenhouse, you or Claire. When the frame went up, you looked just like she did—so happy you could bust."

"I was."

"So was I." He'd never forget that moment. Or this one—Nell smiling at him across the tiny kitchen table, her hair piled on top of her head to get it out of the way while she made coffee and toast. For him. His chest tightened.

She reached over and touched his hand, her forehead creased. "You okay?"

"I just... you're... beautiful."

Her expression softened. "Thank you." She held his gaze. Then she glanced at his plate. "Eat your toast."

"Yes, Miss O'Connor." Smiling, he picked up one of the triangles.

"I didn't mean it like that." She looked adorably flustered. "I just know you have to—"

The sound of a text on his phone was loud in the quiet kitchen. He checked the screen. *Call me if you can.* "It's Jake." He stood. "Sorry. I need to call him. He wouldn't contact me unless it's important."

"By all means. I can put your coffee in a thermos."

"No need. I'll only be a minute."

Jake answered on the first ring. "Hope I didn't interrupt."

"Nope. What's—"

"Henri just called. A reservation request has come in from Fran and Bud Lassiter."

His stomach twisted. "*Damn* him."

"She can tell them she's booked."

"All summer?"

"It could happen."

"They might just find a different place to stay and come anyway. Claire said my mom wanted to visit after school let out, but my dad was super busy and didn't see how he could get away."

"Probably because he planned to use his vacation time to take my mother on a cruise."

"You know that?"

"No, I made it up, but that's how he's worked things in the past." Bitterness laced his words. "Look, this is your call, since it involves Claire. Now that I think about it, Henri can't tell them we're booked. Claire would be over the moon if they stayed in a guest cabin for a few days."

"I can't believe he has the cojones to—"

"Can't you? I totally believe it. The guy has solid brass ones. He thinks he can get away with this like he's gotten away with everything else."

"And it looks like he will, doesn't it?"

"Yeah, it sure does. I'll tell Henri to confirm their reservation. We'll talk soon."

"Wait. What dates are they asking for?"

"Next Friday through Monday morning."

"Son of a—"

"No, son of a bastard. Or rather, sons. You and me, little brother. We both drew the short straw. I'm off to check on the raptors. See ya."

"Later, bro." He disconnected and looked around for Nell.

She stood a short distance away, her arms folded and her expression sad. So very sad.

He cleared his throat. "My parents are coming."

"I figured that out." Unfolding her arms, she came toward him. "I'm sorry."

"Me, too." He tucked his phone in his pocket and gathered her close.

She hugged him tight, nestling her face against his chest. "Your heart's going very fast."

"Because I'm ready to beat the tar out of him. How the *hell* can he—" No point in finishing that rant. Jake was right. His dad had always done whatever he wanted without suffering any consequences. Why stop now?

"When are they coming?"

"Next weekend. Friday through Monday."

"I'll be glad to help you deal with this if you need me to."

"I don't want you anywhere near that bastard."

She glanced up. "I'm not sure you'll be able to get away with that. Claire will want to show off her setup, her uncles and aunts, even me and Val."

"You're right." His gut twisted. "And everyone will be forced to play nice because they love Claire."

"And because they want to support you." She cupped his face in both hands. "So do I. If you'll let me."

Taking her hands in his, he brushed kisses over her fingers and held her gaze. "I'd be a fool not to."

"Yeah, you would." She stepped back and pulled her hands free. "Now get out of here. And take your toast with you. You can eat it on the way."

"I will." She'd made it and he'd eat it. Stacking the triangles together, he glanced at the mug of coffee which she'd also made. "Maybe I should take a thermos, after all."

"Sorry, but I wasn't thinking straight when I offered. You'd have to explain to Claire where you got the thermos."

"Oh."

"I'm assuming she doesn't know we spent the night together."

"I don't think so. That's something I wanted to talk about—how I should handle the subject if the time comes when she figures it out."

"Okay. We'll discuss it later." She made a shooing motion with her hands. "Go, go."

He backed toward the door. "I thought you might have some insights about age-appropriate ways to explain sexuality. Being a teacher and all."

"I'm no expert, but—we can talk when there's more time. Bye, Zeke."

"Bye." He couldn't stand it. Storming back across the room, he cupped the back of her head with his free hand and kissed her, hard and fast. "That's better." Turning on his heel, he walked straight to the door, grabbing his Stetson from an end table as he passed by.

Hat on and kiss bestowed, he glanced back one last time. "I love it when you smile like that."

"Your kisses make me happy."

"Good, because you'll be getting a lot more of them." He touched two fingers to the brim of his hat. "See you soon."

He ate the toast in three bites on the way to his truck. He took the residential streets at the required limit, but once he hit the two-lane out of town, he ignored the signs and boogied, watching for critters and cops as he drove.

He encountered neither and pulled up in front of Henri's place on the dot. Not too shabby, all things considered. Bounding up to the porch, he crossed it in two strides, rapped on the door and went on in. Henri was expecting him.

Claire raced out of the kitchen. "Dad! Gramma Frannie and Grampa Bud are coming to stay at the ranch!"

He acted surprised. "They are? That's great!" He almost choked on the words, but he got them out. "When?"

"They'll be here next *Friday*. Gramma Henri says she'll rearrange your work schedule so we can pick them up in Great Falls." She hopped up and down. "I can't wait, I can't wait!"

Henri walked out of the kitchen and stood behind Claire, her hands on his daughter's shoulders, her eyes filled with sympathy. "Exciting news, huh?" Her tone was enthusiastic but she made a face.

"Yes, ma'am. Very exciting. Well, I'd better take this wrangler and head for the barn. We have critters to feed and stalls to clean, right, pardner?"

"Right, pardner!" She made for the door, grabbed her overnight bag sitting beside it and plucked her hat from the coat tree. Then she gazed at him. "Dad, you have peanut butter on your shirt."

"I do?" He checked, and sure enough, he'd dripped. "Whoops."

Claire sighed and shook her head. "I know exactly what you did."

Henri's eyes widened.

Stay cool, dude. "Oh, you do, do you?"

"Since I wasn't there, you didn't bother to fix yourself a real breakfast. Instead you made toast, ate it too fast and washed it down with coffee. Am I right?"

"More or less."

"I thought so. After we finish barn chores, we need to go back to the bunkhouse so you can get some real food into you."

"Good idea." He glanced at Henri, who'd ducked her head, no doubt to hide her grin. "Thanks so much for keeping Claire last night, Henri."

She looked up, her eyes sparkling with amusement. "You're welcome. Did you have a nice time?"

"Yes, ma'am." He didn't have to fake his response to that question. "I had a wonderful time."

22

Keeping Zeke's secret from Val wasn't an issue over the weekend. Nell didn't hear from her friend, not even a text. Either things had gone exceedingly well with Teague or truly awful. Either way, Val might need some space.

At least she didn't have to worry about saying the wrong thing over a cup of coffee or a glass of wine. On the other hand, she struggled to find a distraction that filled the hole left by Zeke.

Laundry, cleaning and walks through the neighborhood weren't cutting it. She loved to read, but she couldn't sit still long enough to get into the story.

She missed him like crazy. He didn't text and that made sense. Claire was shadowing him this summer so she'd always be around. Hobbies had never been Nell's thing, but maybe that needed to change. She couldn't spend the entire summer pining for that cowboy.

At last Monday arrived, along with a text from Val asking if she could come over early. She wanted a chance to talk about Teague before they picked up the girls for the riding lesson.

Did she have good news or bad? No telling from her text, but the minute Nell opened the door, her friend's glowing face gave her the answer. "You had a good time."

"We had a *fabulous* time. Friday night was so amazing that he asked me to spend the weekend at the ranch, which is why I was out of touch."

"Exciting!" Was she envious that they were free to do that? Maybe a little.

"You have no idea. We stayed at his house, which is very cozy, but we had the whole ranch to ourselves. Ed was at a barrel racing event and her cook had the weekend off. It was so cool to be all alone out there."

"But didn't he have stuff to do?"

"Oh, sure. I just followed him around and helped where I could, like feeding the horses and cleaning the stalls."

"You shoveled horse poop?"

"It's not so bad, and I got to ogle Teague working with his shirt off."

"I see." She smiled. Yep, pea-green with envy. Working alongside a shirtless Zeke would be a dream come true.

"Mostly we had sex. Even outside one time, which I *never* thought I'd do, but since nobody was around, why not?"

"Indeed, why not?" She bopped the green-eyed monster on the head. Time to be happy for her friend. "I assume you two will continue seeing each other?"

"Oh, definitely. Now that Ed's back home, I'm invited to dinner at her place tonight. I've seen her in barrel-racing demonstrations with the Babes but I've never met her. She sounds really interesting."

"I can't wait to hear how that goes."

"I'll let you know. It's fascinating how this has worked out. Teague's been here all along and somehow I missed seeing him. You'd think we would have ended up at the Moose on the same night at least once, but we didn't."

"Timing is everything."

"You're right." She smiled. "Timing and a little help from Claire and her buddies."

"Speaking of that, they'll be looking for evidence that their devious plan worked."

"And they'll find it. There's no fooling those little devils. You and Zeke haven't, so I doubt we can."

"But you don't have to give them extra ammunition."

"Right. Teague and I are taking a page out of yours and Zeke's book—no lingering touches, no secret smiles. They'll still figure we're together, but we'll be on our best behavior."

Nell picked up the tote of water bottles, her purse and her sunglasses. "It's time to gather up those little chicks. Ready?"

"I am. I just had to fill you in before we left."

"Good thing you did, although I'm at least as smart as those girls. I'd have figured it out." She started for the door.

"Yeah, but you shouldn't have to. You're my buddy. I wanted you to be informed." She followed her out to the porch and waited while Nell locked the door. "How did things go with you and Zeke, by the way?"

"Terrific. So terrific I ended up missing him a lot the past couple of days." She started down the porch steps.

"Aww. And here I am raving about my long weekend with Teague."

"Rave on, girlfriend. Don't tone down your excitement on my account."

"Okay, but I can be a little more sensitive about it."

"Nah, I'm fine. Although I'll admit I'm super-excited to see him today." So excited that she'd backed her SUV out of the garage so it would be ready and waiting in the driveway. She'd have to be careful that she didn't spend the whole lesson making puppy eyes at the guy.

She climbed into the driver's seat and waited for Val to get in and buckle up. "Oh, and the big news—Zeke found out Saturday morning that his mom and dad are coming next weekend." She started the car. "They've reserved one of the guest cabins at the Buckskin."

"Hey, that's wonderful! Do they know he's dating you?"

"If they don't, they'll find out." She backed out and headed down the street. "Claire will make sure of it."

"I predict they'll be thrilled that he's found somebody nice after the way his ex-wife treated him."

"Maybe, but they're mostly coming to see Claire and Zeke. It's not like he and I are planning to set up house." Driving to the corner, she turned right. Tatum was their first stop.

"I know, but I'll bet they'll like knowing he's not permanently scarred by that disastrous marriage."

"I guess." Except he was scarred. But he might not have been, if he hadn't been disillusioned a second time by his father's lies. Hard to come bouncing back after a one-two punch like that.

* * *

Getting through the riding lesson without making a fool of herself was tough. She'd likely overcompensated by making sure she and Zeke didn't accidentally touch. At all. She kept her conversations with him brief and rarely made eye contact.

Once she caught herself staring at him like a groupie in the presence of a rock star. She quickly looked away. Was he facing the same dilemma? Probably.

But he wore his manly Stetson pulled low over his eyes. The brim shaded his face and helped disguise his expression. Her riding helmet was no help.

At the end of the lesson, she and Val had a moment alone in the tack room as they carried their saddles in.

Val hoisted hers on the wooden stand. "That was challenging."

"Carrying the saddle in?"

"Playing it cool for the benefit of the girls."

"Tell me about it."

Val glanced at her. "You looked tense. At least Teague and I have the freedom to see each other whenever we want, but you don't have that luxury."

"Zeke feels like one night is all he can justify. I get that. But it would almost be easier if I didn't have these riding lessons. I can see, but I can't touch."

"How will his parents' visit affect things?"

"I don't know. They might want Claire to stay overnight with them, but I'm not counting on it. She likes being with her dad."

"And so do you."

"She comes first. And she should. I just... miss him. I had no idea I'd miss him this much."

"Sounds like you've been bitten by the love bug."

"Can't afford to be." She smiled at Val. "But you go right ahead, girlfriend."

"No way. We're just having fun. I made sure we had that understanding from the get-go. And he—" She turned as Claire came in. "Hey, sunshine! Whatcha need?"

"Just the grooming tote." She grinned. "Bet you and Miss O'Connor were talking about your dates."

Val widened her eyes in fake surprise. "Would we do that?"

"Yes. Yes, you would." Giggling, she hurried out of the tack room, likely to report to her cohorts.

Val gazed after her. "It's all rainbows and unicorns for that girl. She thinks we're living a fairy tale."

"It's more likely she hopes we are. You can't blame her for wanting to believe in that."

"No, I sure can't, poor kid."

"We'd better get back out there. A couple of gentlemen need our attention."

Val grinned. "Zeke and Teague?"

"Butch and Sundance."

"I like those guys, but I wouldn't mind wiping Teague down, instead."

Nell laughed. "I hear you."

The grooming didn't take long. After the horses were turned out to romp in the pasture, Nell brought out the satchel of water bottles from the tack room and encouraged everyone to finish up whatever was left. She'd added a silver one for Teague.

He finished off his water and approached Zeke. "What would it take to get you to trade me? I covet that snazzy pink one."

Zeke shook his head. "Dream on, cowboy. You couldn't handle this awesome color."

"Try me."

"Sorry. This is now my signature shade. I might even paint my truck to match this water bottle."

"Dad!" Claire looked horrified. "Wranglers don't drive pink trucks!"

"You never know. I might start a trend." He winked at Nell.

Dear God, why did he have to be so appealing? In a few minutes, she'd have to round up her charges, pile into her SUV and drive away. Maintaining her distance while in his presence was tough, but leaving him would be worse. "Hand over your water bottles, gang. We need to get going."

Zeke held up his. "What if I want to keep it?"

She glanced at him. "Well, I guess—"

"I don't think that's a good idea, Dad." Claire's expression was adorably earnest. "Miss O'Connor came up with a good system. We need to stick with the system."

"Ah, I see your point." He came over and handed the bottle to Nell. "Thank you."

"You're welcome." She risked looking into his warm brown eyes, gulped and dropped her gaze. "Guess that's it, then. Let's all thank Mr. Lassiter and Mr. Sullivan for another great session."

After a flurry of high-pitched thank yous, the girls hurried toward the car. Claire went with them so she could see them off, and Teague escorted Val.

Nell gave Zeke a quick smile before turning to follow them.

"Nell."

"Yes?" She swung around, heart thumping.

"I need to talk with you for a minute." He closed the short distance between them.

"Okay." She clutched the tote in both hands to keep from reaching for him.

"The Brotherhood's having an overnight at the bunkhouse on Thursday and the Babes will have their usual monthly bash up at Henri's. Both events were shifted to this week so everyone can discuss how to handle my folks' visit."

"Good idea, but why are you telling—"

"I'm getting to that." He kept his voice down. "I'd like you to participate in the discussion around the fire pit, if you're willing. I value your input."

She frowned. "I'm willing, but how can you have a discussion with Claire around?"

"She won't be. On Brotherhood overnights, she goes to the slumber party at Kate's cottage. That's become quite a thing and she loves it. They all cram in there—ladies and kids—although now it's warm enough for some to sleep on the porch."

"Then sure, I'll be happy to sit in on the fire pit discussion. What time?"

"Come about six. We'll have dinner and brainstorm."

"All right. Thanks for asking me." She backed away. "I'd better get over to the—"

"One other thing." His voice sounded raspy.

"What?"

"After the discussion, if you want..." His breath hitched. "I can follow you back to your place."

She gulped. "I didn't see that coming."

"Would that work for you?"

"You know it would."

His chest heaved. "I'm glad. I miss you."

"Same here." Mesmerized by the intensity in his eyes, she couldn't get her feet to move.

"They're calling for you."

"Right." She hadn't heard a thing. Tearing her gaze from his, she turned and fled. Another second and she would have kissed him.

23

Zeke paced the parking area in front of the bunkhouse a little after six on Thursday night, his phone in his hand. Just about everybody was here.

Matt, Rafe and Leo were out back tending the fire pit. Jake and Nick were fixing dinner. Once Nell arrived, he'd lend a hand in the preparations, either in the kitchen or the fire pit. Might be silly to wait out here until she showed up, but he didn't trust himself to cook or mind the fire just now. He'd likely burn the food, himself or both.

He always looked forward to spending time with her, but now that his dad had ramped up the stakes, she had become a steady anchor in a topsy-turvy world.

Tonight's gathering hadn't been his idea, but he'd been totally in favor. Creating a game plan for this parental visit was a practical move. Creating an opportunity to be with Nell added another positive to the evening.

He'd rather have picked her up so he could drive her back instead of following her home. But the slumber party didn't officially start until six. He'd dropped Claire off at Kate's right on time and then quickly come back here, thinking Nell might have beat him.

The sound of an engine put him on alert. No, not the SUV. More of a growl than a purr. Garrett's truck came around the bend in the road and pulled in next to Zeke's. Garrett climbed out. "Not here, yet?"

"Nope. But I told her *about* six. It's not like she's late."

"She'll be here." Garrett ambled over. "I just dropped Anna and Georgie off at Kate's. That place is jumping."

"I imagine Claire's a big part of that. She's been on springs lately, between her grandparents arriving tomorrow and this party tonight."

Garrett studied him. "How are you holding up?"

"Okay."

"Tell that to someone who doesn't know you. It took a good two months for you to begin to relax. Now you're wound tight again. I hate that your dad's doing this to you."

"At least I'm not alone in this fight."

"And that's huge. I can't tell you how many times I've thanked my lucky stars I landed at the Buckskin."

"Same here. Even if it was my rotten father's suggestion."

"A broken clock's right twice a day."

"Yeah. Anyway, he sent me because of Jake. He didn't know I'd have the entire Buckskin gang watching my back."

"Plus Nell. I'm glad you invited her tonight."

"Seemed like the thing to do, considering how she feels about Claire."

"And you."

Guilt pricked him. "I think a lot of her, too." He nudged a pebble with the toe of his boot.

"Too bad you can't see more of each other."

"Uh-huh."

"There is a solution, you know."

He glanced up. "Have you been talking to Henri?"

"About what?"

"She's offered to rent a guest cabin to Nell at whatever rate she's paying for her house in town. Did you suggest—"

"I did not. It's news to me. I was thinking you and Claire could move to Nell's house, but I like this option better."

"I'm not in favor of either one. I'd never ask Claire to move to town."

"But this way she wouldn't have to."

"No, she'd end up leaving the bunkhouse and she's in heaven there. Nell loves that she's within walking distance of her school. They both have the perfect setup. I'm not messing with that."

Garrett smiled. "Because you're not desperate enough, yet."

"Sometimes I am. But then I think of what's best for Claire and Nell. That cools my jets."

"I'll check in with you in a week or so. See if your jets are still cool."

"They will be."

Garrett gave him a knowing look. "Don't forget, I've been where you are and I've been where you're gonna be before long. I can see the signs."

"Maybe I'm more mentally tough than you." And more paranoid about making that kind of far-reaching decision.

"Maybe you are tougher than I am. But it's easy to talk big when she's not standing right in front of you. And speaking of that, I hear her car."

He did, too. Adrenaline pumped through his system.

"I'll leave so you can have a little time alone with her. I should help cook, anyway."

"Thanks, buddy."

As Garrett headed inside, Nell's white SUV came around the bend. He beckoned her over to a parking spot where she wouldn't get blocked in.

By the time she'd shut off the motor, he had her door open. "Hi."

"Hi, yourself." She flipped open the buckle of her seatbelt and slid out of the car into his outstretched arms. "God, I've missed—"

He cut her off with a kiss that made him groan with its sweetness. How had he lasted since Saturday morning without this? *It's easy to talk big when she's not standing right in front of you.* And kissing the heck out of him.

Winding her arms around his neck, she leaned in close and slackened her jaw. He thrust his tongue into her hot mouth and his hand into the wild luxury of her unbound hair. He was instantly aroused. Insanity. They probably shouldn't be doing this, but he couldn't seem to stop. She tasted like—

She wiggled away from him, her breathing ragged. "I hear a truck."

He did, too, damn it. "CJ." Did they have time to slip into the stand of pines nearby? He wasn't ready to stop kissing her. Not yet. He grabbed her hand. "Let's go over—"

Resisting him, she smiled. "Hearing the truck reminds me that I'm not here to make out with you."

He sighed. She'd worn the pretty flowered dress and soft white sweater from the day of the field trip. He wanted that tempting body pressed against him one more time.

"You should see your face." Her smile broadened into a grin. "You look like one of my third graders after his scoop of ice cream fell off the cone onto the sidewalk."

"Which is exactly how I feel." He squeezed her hand and let go. "And I haven't had that particular flavor of ice cream for a very long time."

"Five days."

"Five days, twelve hours and..." He glanced at the phone still in his hand. "Forty-seven minutes." He looked up. "Not that I've been counting."

"And if your parents weren't coming tomorrow, we wouldn't be able to—"

"I know. It's called making lemonade out of lemons." He turned as CJ's truck pulled in. "That's the last member of the Brotherhood. Let's get this party started."

When they walked over to greet CJ, he regarded them with a twinkle in his gaze. "A bit of lipstick transfer going on there, kids."

Zeke rubbed his mouth. "Is it gone?"

"Yeah. It wasn't much, but I have an eye for those things." He started toward the front door.

"You and the entire Brotherhood." Zeke put his arm around Nell's waist as they followed CJ. "Judging from the stories, you guys were merciless when you all lived in the bunkhouse. A guy couldn't get away with anything."

"Neither can you," CJ said. "You might not have us living with you, but you have Claire."

"Isn't that the truth." He made a mental note to tell Nell about the peanut butter. It would make her laugh.

He ushered her into the bunkhouse just as Jake, Nick and Garrett announced that dinner was ready. He and Nell helped them carry the feast out to the table near the fire pit.

When the Buckskin women were involved in a summer gathering, bouquets of flowers decorated the table. CJ brought out his guitar and Leo set up his projectors to fill the trees with sparkling lights.

Even without all that, Nell commented on how cozy everything looked with the fire, the table loaded with food and the semi-circle of Adirondack chairs waiting for them when they finished their meal.

"Usually it's a little more festive out here," Zeke said. "But tonight's more like a business meeting."

"Serious business, little brother." Jake set a huge platter of fried chicken in the middle of the table.

"Then why didn't you invite the Babes? I figured if you needed them here back in February to sort out Garrett's situation, you'd want them here tonight."

"We considered it." Matt tossed one more log on the fire, picked up his bottle of cider from a chummy stump and walked over to the table. "But having the Babes requires going full out and we didn't feel like we have the bandwidth."

"And sometimes," Jake added, "you get more ideas if each group deliberates separately. On top of that, they love their monthly bash. They might even get inspired during their karaoke session."

"Their *what*?" Nell stared at Jake.

"I keep forgetting you don't know these things, Nell. My apologies. Ever since Charley died, they've met once a month, usually on Thursday night, to eat and drink whatever they feel like and sing karaoke."

"I definitely hadn't heard that. I'm surprised Claire didn't tell me."

"Oh, she wouldn't," Jake said. "It's privileged info, only known by the inner circle."

"Am I part of the inner circle, now?"

Jake smiled at her. "Yes, ma'am. Welcome to the Buckskin gang."

"Wow. Thank you."

Zeke suffered another stab of guilt at the delight in her voice. She was thrilled to be included. Clearly it was because of her connection to him, even though he'd staked no claim, made no promises.

He had, however, asked her to be here tonight. Evidently the Brotherhood had looked at that and figured it was a sign that she belonged in the group. Henri's offer of a cabin could have stemmed from the same thing. He was glad she was here, but the implications had sailed right over his clueless head.

When they took their places on the picnic benches on either side of the table, he grabbed the end seat, putting him on Claire's right. Jake sat on her left. Zeke glanced over at him. "Did you ask Millie if she wanted to come?"

"I did." Jake dished himself potato salad and passed the bowl to Nell. "But she's too angry to discuss the problem without blowing up. It's not fair to say all redheads have a temper, but Millie fits the profile."

Matt laughed and helped himself to some chicken. "I'll vouch for that. Probably wise of her not to come. We need to assess this as calmly as we can. I doubt it'll be easy for either you or Zeke, but we're gonna give it our best shot."

"And I appreciate that." Zeke put food on his plate, although his appetite was gone.

"The bottom line is Claire," Jake said. "What I feel about this is secondary."

"Agreed." Zeke took a deep breath and let it out, trying to ease the tension bottled up inside him. "But I need to get this off my chest. That bastard is counting on us to welcome him, or at least tolerate him because we love Claire. He's using our devotion to her to get what he wants, a visit with his grandchild. I thought I couldn't hate him any more than do, but I was wrong."

24

Nell longed to wrap her arms around Zeke. Since that wasn't doable, she laid her hand gently on his thigh, giving him the option of holding her hand under the table.

He took it, sliding his fingers through hers in a firm grip. "I have a request regarding tomorrow's pickup at the airport. The plane lands a few minutes past noon. I'm going with Claire, and I could use backup."

She squeezed his hand. "I'll go."

"I wish you could." His gaze was gentle. "But you can't."

"Why not? I want to help."

"And I'd love to take you, but if you're standing with me and Claire at the arrival gate, my mom will convince herself we're as good as engaged."

"One question, little brother." Jake set down his cider bottle. "You fixin' to put your backup on the roof? You'll be squeezed tight with your folks, Claire and you, without—"

"Forgot to say Henri's loaning me her truck. That leaves room for one more."

"That'll be me, then. Providing you and me standing together won't make your mother hear wedding bells. Don't want to confuse the issue."

A few snorts of laughter followed that comment. Even Zeke smiled. "Thanks, Jake. It's a noble offer, but you don't have to sacrifice yourself."

"It's not a sacrifice. It's extremely self-serving. I was planning to go, anyway. Figured I'd caravan behind you, is all."

"You don't have to do this, bro."

"I figure I do. I'll need to face the devil sooner or later."

"Yeah, but—"

"This would work for me, little brother. I'd be forced to be civil because Claire's right there loving on him. There's a much better chance I won't follow my first instinct and deck him."

"I'm worried I might do that, too. It's why I wanted somebody to come with me. Just not you. What if we both snap?"

"That's why I should go." Garrett glanced at him from across the table. "I'll keep both of you from doing something you'll regret. And I'll be protective coloring."

Zeke stared at him. "You'll be what?"

"Your mom doesn't know Jake's your half-brother, right?"

"Right."

"Claire calling him uncle won't be a big deal because she'll call me uncle, too."

Zeke nodded. "Good thinking, but it could be a tight squeeze on the way back."

"We'd fit, right, Jake?"

"Sure. I'll sit in your lap."

"Never mind. I'll just drive myself. Anybody want to ride with me?"

"Hell, yeah, I do." Leo grinned. "You never take me anywhere anymore."

Nick looked at Rafe. "We should go. The more uncles the better."

"Definitely."

"Hang on," Matt said. "Aren't you forgetting—"

"Damn straight," CJ said. "They're forgetting us. You and me. We're uncles, too, y'know."

"That may be, but all the *uncles* are also Buckskin wranglers. Everyone can't go running off to Great Falls to meet this plane. We don't even know how long we'd be gone. There could be delays, lost luggage, you name it."

CJ sighed. "But it would be so cool if we could. Imagine if we dressed up real nice, like we did for the field trip, and stood there with a sign."

"A sign would be super," Jake said. "I can see it now." Spreading his fingers, he swept his hand across an imaginary banner. "*GO HOME YOU LOUSY BASTARD.*"

Zeke chuckled. Then the chuckle turned into a belly laugh. He fished in his back pocket for his bandana so he could wipe his eyes.

Jake gazed at him and shook his head. "Pressure must've got to him. Poor boy's having a fit."

"Sorry." Zeke cleared his throat and stuffed the bandana back in his pocket. "That was a great image, big brother. Too bad we can't do it."

"Maybe we can't make that sign," Garrett said, "but we should all go to the airport and line up in a show of strength. We need to let this man know he's dealing with a lot more than two angry sons. He's dealing with the Brotherhood."

Nell glanced at Zeke, who was clearly speechless. His stunned expression brought tears to her eyes. "I don't have any say in this." She cleared the huskiness from her throat. "But I think Garrett's right. You all need to go. I realize you can't leave Henri to run the ranch by herself, but maybe—"

"It won't just be Henri." Matt reached for his phone. "Don't know why I didn't think of it before. We'll call in the Babes."

* * *

For the trip back to town, Zeke suggested they use their hands-free option and communicate by phone during the drive.

"That'll be different." Nell accepted his help getting into her SUV. "We don't get to chat on the phone."

"We sure don't, and I've wanted to dozens of times. But Claire's always there and I couldn't say… it wouldn't be…"

"Private."

"Exactly. I've considered going outside to call you after she's asleep, but I don't want her to wake up and find me gone." He tapped on the screen. "Calling you now."

Her phone played the refrain from *Head Over Boots*. Whoops. She tapped her phone. "Hi,

Zeke." She hadn't factored in that he'd find out the ringtone she'd assigned to him. Normally he wouldn't have a reason to hear it.

"Hi, Nell. *Head Over Boots,* huh?" He was smiling. Even his eyes were smiling.

"I've always liked it."

"So it has nothing to do with the fact it's the first song we danced to?"

"It might. What about my ringtone? Is it generic or—"

"Not generic. I'll play it for you later." He motioned to her seat belt. "Buckle up. The sooner we get out of here, the sooner we'll be at your place." He backed away and closed her door.

Sticking her phone in its holder on her dash, she turned the ignition key, put the car in gear, and backed out. "Am I leading?"

"Yes, ma'am." He chuckled. "Don't speed."

"Touché." She started down the dirt road. The headlights of Zeke's truck appeared in her rearview mirror. "If you were leading, how fast would you go?"

"Too fast. That's why you're leading."

"Sure is dark out here at night." She switched on her high beams.

"And I love that. You can see the stars way better than you can in town."

"I didn't think to look up while I was out by the fire pit. I was too involved in the conversation."

"Next time you come out, I'll make sure you look at them. It's like some giant hand spilled sugar on black satin."

What a great opening. She'd meant to surprise him, but a little teasing might be more fun. "Or a black satin nightgown?"

"Even better image." He paused. "Was that a random comment?"

"Not really." She reached the paved part of the ranch road and increased her speed.

"Been shopping again, Miss O'Connor?"

"Maybe."

His breath hitched. "What's the plan, pretty lady?"

"I'm not sure it's safe to tell you. You might drive into a ditch."

"You'll have to tell me sometime. Otherwise we'll be going with my plan."

"Which is?"

"Get you naked and in bed ASAP. I want you something fierce."

A flush spread over every inch of her. "I want you, too. Maybe we should forget about the nightgown." Also the candles, the perfumed sheets, and the hide-and-seek game with his condom stash. "I can save it for another time. We don't have to—"

"Oh, yeah, we do. I'm forming an image in my head and my plan just got shelved. We're going with yours."

"You're sure?"

"I am. Certain parts of me are *very* into this plan."

"Okay, then." She braked at the stop sign before turning onto the two-lane highway. Nobody coming from either direction. She pulled out. A couple seconds later, his headlights were behind her again.

"How do you want to work it?"

Her pulse rate ratcheted up. "When we get there, stay in the truck until I text you to come in."

"Got it." A pause. "What's the nightgown look like?"

"Don't you want to be surprised?"

"I want to anticipate."

The sexy roughness in his voice tightened her nipples and dampened her panties. "The straps are thin. The bodice is cut in a deep vee edged with black lace."

He made a low humming sound. "Go on."

"It nips in at the waist and flares out around my hips. The hem is trimmed with lace, too."

"How short?"

"Very."

"Can I see your—"

"Not *that* short." Her blood heated.

"What if you turn around and lean over?"

She sucked in a breath. "What are you thinking?"

"Everything." His tone softened. "I want to know you, Nell. Every special place on your beautiful body. What gets you hot, where you're ticklish, what happens when I stroke your—hey, slow down, lady."

"Slow down? I'm only doing..." She gasped. "Eighty?" She took her foot off the accelerator. "And you were keeping up with me!"

His laughter was deep and rich. "I'm doing my best. You're the one buying flavored oils and sexy lingerie. What's next? Velvet handcuffs?"

"No! I can't imagine ever—"

"You sure about that?" His tone held a subtle challenge.

He inspired honesty and she gave it to him. The phone made it easier, though. "You're the most exciting man I've ever known."

"Nice to hear."

"You have an amazing body and a sense of adventure, which thrills the heck out of me and makes me want to... expand my horizons."

"I see velvet handcuffs in our future."

"Have you ever tried them?"

"No, but I've never made love to anyone like you, either. Every time is different, special. I don't know how you do that, but—"

"It's not me, it's us. It's like we've found—" She caught herself before she finished the sentence with *the right person.* She hurried on. "I know this isn't going anywhere, *can't* go anywhere. That said, I... treasure being with you."

Silence. Damn. Even with censoring herself, she'd said too much. "Zeke, please don't think that I'm trying to—"

"Nell." His voice was thick with emotion. "You're the treasure. I don't deserve all that you've given and all you continue to give. I... I wish I could..." The rest was too soft to understand, but might have been Zeke swearing under his breath.

"Don't torture yourself," she murmured. "You have a lot on your plate right now. Let me be the dessert." She pulled into her driveway and shut off the motor. "I'll text you when I'm ready."

His truck glided in next to the curb. The engine rumbled for a moment and then was still.

The lights flicked off. His voice came through her phone, low and urgent. "Hurry."

25

Zeke unsnapped his seat belt, leaned back and drew in a deep, cleansing breath. *Nell.* Every nerve and muscle in his body ached for her.

His heart ached the worst. Her words had tipped the scales tonight, nudged Matt into a realization he hadn't considered. The result? The Brotherhood would stand united at the arrival gate tomorrow, a force to be reckoned with. What an incredible gift.

She wouldn't want to take credit for making that happen. She'd likely describe her part as inconsequential and insist that Garrett had made the pivotal speech. Maybe so, but nobody had leaped in to second his motion.

Nell had done that. And he loved her for it. He groaned aloud. He loved her, damn it! For so many reasons—her affection for Claire and her posse, her willingness to accept every single limitation he imposed on their relationship, her eagerness to add spice to their sex life.

But uttering words of love carried an obligation. A man who said those words had better be prepared to take next steps. He wouldn't have a clue where to put his feet. Land mines were everywhere. He'd set off too many in the past.

Sticking with what he had was the safest bet. The ranch was a healing place for Claire. For him, too. It offered the life they craved and the close family connections they'd soaked up like sponges from day one.

Making any change to that setup carried a greater risk than he wanted to take. Nell had accepted this arrangement. He'd best do the same.

His phone pinged. Picking it up, he tapped the screen. No words, just a series of pictures—candles glowing, sheets turned back, selfies highlighting her hair fanned out on the pillow, her abundant cleavage and her creamy thighs beneath the lace-trimmed negligee.

Tossing the phone on the seat, he laid his hat on the dash, left the truck and lengthened his stride, wincing as the fly of his jeans punished him for his lusty thoughts. His feelings for Nell transcended mere sex, but that didn't mean her sensuality was a side issue.

Right now, it was everything. Hormones saturated his brain and prompted him to shuck his boots and socks at the door and pull off his shirt on the way down the hall. Flickering candlelight danced on the floorboards outside her bedroom doorway.

Unbuckling his belt, he stripped it off and dropped it as he stepped inside. The clatter merged with his quick inhale. She lay stretched out on the chalk-white sheets, her head propped on her hand, the sheen of black satin barely covering her tempting body.

He gulped. "I could come just looking at you."

"But you won't let yourself." Her voice was a soft purr. "I know you better than that. You like to prolong the moment while you drive me crazy."

"Yes, ma'am." He unzipped his jeans as he approached the bed. "I sure do."

"But this time it's my turn."

He paused, heart thudding. "Oh?"

She scooted over and patted the bed. "Take off those jeans and come on down here."

He kept his gaze on her as he shoved down his jeans and briefs and kicked them away. "Happy to. Just let me get—" He reached for the drawer where he'd stashed his supply of condoms.

"They're not there."

He paused. "Where are they?"

"Somewhere else."

"Why?"

"Because I don't want you rushing to put one on. I have some other things in mind." She held out her hand. "Come lie down. On your back."

Moisture pooled in his mouth. He knew where this was going, and he wanted what she was offering. That activity hadn't fit with their other sessions because he'd always been quick to roll on a condom.

Now she'd hidden them. Much as he relished the idea of what she had in mind, he wanted to know where she'd tucked those little raincoats. "Where are they?"

"I'll tell you after I have some fun." She wiggled her fingers. "I want to play."

"And I want to let you." He took her hand and sat on the bed. "But you need to tell me where you put the condoms, so I have one handy."

"So you can grab it before you come?"

"Right."

"I was hoping to give you the whole experience."

His chest tightened. He hadn't been loved that way in... years. That kind of trust hadn't existed in his marriage.

"You don't want me to?"

He gazed at her and the bands around his chest loosened a bit. "I do."

"Then you don't need a—"

"I want it there on the bedside table."

"Why?"

"Because nine years ago, I was out of my head with lust, couldn't find one and had sex without it. I don't regret that for one second, even though it caused me to marry the wrong woman. But that's why I'm fantatical about—"

"I understand. Hang on." She rolled to the other side of the bed and reached between the mattress and box springs. "Here are two."

"Just two?" He laid them on the nightstand.

"The others are tucked in various places. I..." She gave him a sheepish smile. "It's the elementary teacher in me. I like games."

"You're adorable."

"I wouldn't have done it if I'd known. So now you have access to a couple, but I don't want you to stop me and grab a condom. Will you promise not to?"

His heart thundered. He was putting her in his hands, literally. And in her mouth, to be precise. She'd asked for his complete surrender. He took a ragged breath. "I promise."

"Good." She glanced at his stiff cock and licked her lips. "Lie down."

He stretched out on the bed, anticipation tinged with anxiety flowed like lava through his body. He promised to let go of the reins. Easier said than done.

She straddled his hips, black satin brushing against various parts of his supercharged package. When she leaned over, her breasts threatened to spill out of her gown.

She started slow, with gentle licks and soft kisses. Clenching his jaw, he dug his fingers into the mattress. Could he last more than a few seconds? Would he embarrass himself by coming the minute she closed her lips around his cock?

He would if he watched. He squeezed his eyes shut. Didn't help much. Her warm breath made him shiver. When she took him into her hot mouth, his balls tightened.

Then she began to use her tongue, apply pressure, move a little… ahh. He fought to hold back, panting with the effort. If he stopped her now, he could maintain his dignity. But he'd promised.

His control began to slip. He groaned, grasping for a shred of resistance to the pressure building in his overheated body. Not working. Losing the battle… so good… *so good…*

With a wild cry, he came, helpless in the grip of a climax that roared through him, a tsunami of deafening pleasure. As the pulsing gradually subsided, his ears buzzed and his breath came in tortured gasps.

She stayed with him until he grew quiet. After releasing his cock with great tenderness, she slid up beside him and gave him a deep kiss. He cupped the back of her head and kissed her back. He was drained, yet energized.

Lifting her head, she nestled her cheek against his shoulder. "Thank you."

He huffed in surprise. "You're thanking *me*?"

"You let yourself be vulnerable. I wasn't sure you would."

He wound his arms around her. "I wasn't sure I would, either. But I'm glad I did. I feel... different."

"How?"

"Like I survived going over the falls in a barrel."

She chuckled. "That intense, was it?"

"That might be a slight exaggeration. I wasn't afraid I would die."

"But you were afraid?"

"I was. My life is all about keeping it together. Just now I set myself up to come completely unglued, reduced to a howling, crazy man who barely knows what he's doing."

"But doesn't the same thing happen when we make love?"

"Not if you come first."

"Oh, so you want me to become the howling crazy person so your reaction gets lost in the shuffle."

"That's the sad truth of it." He stroked her hair.

"Well, now that you've gone over the falls in a barrel, think you'll ever want to do it again?"

"Not tonight."

"I wouldn't expect that. But have you conquered your fear?"

"Yes, ma'am." He hesitated. Yeah, he could say it. "As long as I'm with you.

<u>26</u>

Nell's sensual gift to Zeke deepened their connection, adding to the magic as they made love. Although he didn't say the word, his touch and the light in his eyes told her all she needed to know.

They slept a little and he left at dawn, his reluctance obvious. Being with her clearly bolstered his spirits, but his decision to face this family drama without her was the right one.

Sending him off with kisses and smiles, she settled into a day of waiting for news. She'd thrown in a load of laundry and was making a grocery list when Val texted.

Lunch at Gertie's? I desperately need to talk.

Desperately? When she'd bid her friend goodbye after the riding lesson, Val was looking forward to having dinner with Teague at the Choosy Moose.

She typed a quick reply. *Twelve-thirty?*

C U then. No exclamation points, no smiley faces.

Val was an emoji nut. Something was very wrong in her world if she was sending undecorated texts.

Uh-oh. Phone battery was very low. Better charge it. Zeke would likely contact her at some point today or tonight. Oh, yeah, he hadn't played her the ringtone he'd assigned to her, after all. They'd both forgotten. No wonder. They'd been too busy making love to think about ringtones.

Two hours later, she parked in front of Gertie's. Val's little truck sat two spaces down, but Val wasn't in it. She wasn't sitting at one of the two umbrella-topped bistro tables on the sidewalk, either.

The sandwich shop was at its festive best in warm weather, when pots of red geraniums picked up the color of the red-and-white umbrellas. Both tables were taken by folks surrounded by shopping bags, likely tourists.

Val must be inside saving them a place. Visitors flocked to Apple Grove this time of year. Because the summer crowd helped keep local businesses afloat, Nell didn't mind that seating was hard to come by in one of her favorite eateries.

As she started toward the entrance, Val hailed her. Her friend hurried down the sidewalk, a shopping bag in each hand.

She held them up. "I just dropped a wad at Jeans Junction."

"Are they having a sale?" Funny that Val hadn't mentioned it and hadn't thought to invite her.

"No sale. This is therapy."

Val always waited for a sale. "Teague?"

"Yep." Big sunglasses hid her eyes, but her voice quivered. Her gorgeous blond hair, which she usually styled with a brush and blow dryer, looked as if it had been washed and left to dry on its own. "Let's go order."

"My treat." Nell held the door for her.

"You don't have to do that." Val paused. "No seats."

"Let's get stuff to go and take it over to the gazebo."

"That'll work." Misery echoed in every syllable. "Probably better, anyway."

Nell convinced Val to let her pay, probably because Val didn't have the energy to argue. They stood in silence at the pickup window waiting for their order.

Eager to lift the dismal mood that had settled over them, Nell glanced at the bags. "What did you buy?"

"I don't know." Val shrugged. "Jeans, blouses."

Whatever had happened must be *really* bad. Val loved shopping for clothes. She was built like a model, tall and slim. Everything looked good on her.

Eventually their order came up. Nell picked up the cardboard tray that held both sacks and their drinks. Then she led the way out the door and across the street to the grassy square. "Smells good out here."

"Does it?"

"Yeah, especially the grass. Since I grew up in a high-rise, I'm always excited about walking on it and breathing in that tangy smell." She looked over at the gazebo. "Nobody's claimed the steps. There's even a bit of shade. We can sit there."

"Okay."

"Or we can climb up to the roof if you want. I'm sure there's a nice view of the mountains from there."

Val looked over at her. "Very funny."

"I thought so."

She plopped down on the second step from the top and handed Val her sack and her iced tea.

"Thank you. Thank you for buying my lunch. That was sweet." She stared at the sack without opening it. Then she sniffed.

"Oh, Val." Nell put down her sandwich and wrapped an arm around her friend's shoulders. "What happened?"

"He... he proposed!" She choked back a sob. "The dirty rat asked me to marry him!"

It would be hilarious, except it wasn't. "I thought you made yourself clear on that issue."

"I did! So help me, I absolutely did." She pushed her sunglasses to the top of her head, dug in the bag and pulled out a napkin. Then she mopped her face and blew her nose.

"Then why did he propose?"

"He didn't believe me. He thinks I say that to every guy in the beginning. But after we had such a great time together, especially in bed, he figured I was falling for him so he popped the question."

"After a week?"

"He said it wasn't the time that was important, it was the amazing connection." She took a shaky breath and blew her nose again.

"Is he in love with you?"

"He thinks he is. But how can he be? Like you said, it's been a week. Nobody falls in love in a week except in the movies."

"Well, I've heard of a few cases." She'd been involved with Zeke for only two weeks and her heart was definitely on the line. Then again, she'd spent time with him building the greenhouse. She'd been half in love with him after that.

"I can't believe he's done this. He ruined *everything*."

"I take it you're not in love with him."

"Certainly not!"

"Then I have a question."

"What?"

"Don't get mad at me, but... if you're not into him, why are you crying?"

"I'm not in love! I'm furious! I want to punch him in his sexy face. I almost did, too, but I have a mean left hook and I might have broken that beautiful nose."

"I'm glad you restrained yourself."

"It wasn't easy. I reminded him of what I'd said, that I only want a nice guy to have a good time with. He asked why we couldn't have a good time as husband and wife. He doesn't get it."

"So it's over?"

"*So* over, and I hate that because he's got it all—a cute house, a terrific body, sexy moves in bed, good hygiene—" She paused. "You just snorted. What's so funny about good hygiene?"

"Nothing." Nell swallowed her laughter. "It's highly desirable in a partner." And Val was full of it. Whether she wanted to be emotionally involved with Teague or not, she was up to her eyeballs in gooey feelings for that cowboy.

On the other hand, she was so dead-set against making a commitment that she might not recognize love if it bit her on the backside. And if Teague was an inventive lover, it probably had.

"You know what else? Now I have to see him twice a week for the riding lessons."

"I guess you could quit."

"Hell, no, I'm not quitting. I suggested he find someone to take over for him so he wouldn't have to suffer through seeing me twice a week. But he has no intention of doing that. He's attached to those girls."

"And they're attached to him."

"He had the gall to mention that. He even said—get this—that since we both like kids so much, we'd be awesome parents! Can you believe the guy?"

"He has cojones, all right."

"I don't want to think about his cojones, thank you very much."

Nell ducked her head. Giggling was not appropriate. Val was in pain, even though it was self-inflicted. Between Zeke's folks and Val's feud with Teague, this weekend would be a doozy.

27

Jake insisted on giving Claire the front seat on the trip to the airport. Zeke glanced in the rearview mirror as his daughter chattered away, regaling Jake with stories about her beloved Gramma Frannie and Grampa Bud.

Jake was quick with a smile or a comment whenever Claire twisted toward the back seat. The rest of the time he sat in stoic silence, his big hands gripping his knees, his jaw clenched tight.

Zeke wasn't crazy about the stream of praise for Bud, either. He switched on the radio to distract himself and Jake from the litany of Bud's awesomeness. Helped a little.

At some point in the past few hours he'd switched to calling him Bud instead of *my dad*. It was a small act of rebellion that added distance. Clearly Jake had noticed because he'd started doing it, too.

The side-view mirror gave him a glimpse of the gleaming vintage grille of Garrett's refurbished truck. The other six members of the Brotherhood had divided up between Garrett's truck and Matt's shiny black one. Leo and Rafe rode with Garrett. CJ and Nick were with Matt. All three trucks had been washed and detailed.

Every so often Jake turned around and looked through the back window. He was likely as cheered by the caravan as Zeke was. Everyone had taken CJ's suggestion and dressed to the nines. Hats were brushed and boots polished. Zeke wore the black shirt Nell admired so much.

Claire had on her favorite yoked shirt and her newest pair of jeans. Her boots were polished and her hat brushed, too. He'd asked if she wanted to wear the dress Gramma Frannie had sent her for Easter. She'd rejected the idea, announcing that she was a wrangler, now, and wranglers didn't wear frilly dresses.

His mom would be disappointed not to see Claire wearing it, but he didn't push. His daughter had a right to choose. If the dress never came out of the closet, they'd donate it to charity.

They'd hit the halfway point when his tolerance for Bud stories gave out. He switched off the radio. "Hey, sweetie, remember how we sang rounds when we made the drive to Apple Grove in February?"

"I sure do. That was fun!"

He checked in the rearview. "Want to sing rounds with us, Uncle Jake?"

"You bet, little brother."

"Yay!" Claire bounced in her seat. "I'll start us off, then Daddy, then you. I'll point to each of you when it's your turn. Got it?"

Jake smiled. "Got it, Claire-bear."

She giggled. Jake had come up with the rhyming nickname a few weeks ago in reference to her large collection of teddy bears. She clearly loved him to call her that. "You're silly, Uncle Jake."

"Never said I wasn't."

"Do you know Row, Row, Row Your Boat?"

"I believe I do. If I get stuck, I'll just fake it."

"I'll tell it to you." She recited the words slowly. "Row, row, row your boat, gently down the stream. Merrily, merrily, merrily, merrily, life is but a dream. Think you can remember that?"

"I'll do my best."

Zeke checked in the mirror again. Jake's expression had improved a hundred and fifty percent. His eyes had lost their haunted look. The signature Jake twinkle was back.

"When I do this chopping motion with my hand, that means we quit and go to the next song. Otherwise you'll get sick of this one."

"You have more songs?" Jake's expression brightened even more.

"Oh, yeah. A ton of them."

"Excellent."

"Okay, here we go!" Claire belted out the first line, pointed at him and then turned to signal Jake.

Ah, much better. They didn't sound half-bad, either. Jake was clearly into it, adding rowing motions to his backseat performance. They might make it through this part of the trip, after all.

The ride home would be a challenge, though. He and Jake had discussed the seating arrangement. They'd stick Bud at shotgun and put Claire in the back between her Gramma Frannie and Jake.

Bud wasn't exactly a joy to have in the passenger seat, but it was better than making Jake deal with him. The few times Zeke had driven Bud somewhere, he'd spent the time offering unsolicited advice on navigating traffic. Maybe they'd sing rounds on the way back, too.

* * *

The plane was on time. So was the Brotherhood. Matt took charge, organizing the lineup at the base of the escalator and placing Zeke and Claire in the middle. After much discussion, Jake claimed the place on Claire's other side.

Claire was in favor. "He'll be glad to see you, Uncle Jake. He might not get to show it because he doesn't want Gramma Frannie to know, but inside he'll be very happy you're there."

Her innocent evaluation made Zeke's heart hurt. Over the top of Claire's head, he met Jake's gaze. Any amusement left over from singing rounds was gone. The light of battle glowed in his brother's eyes.

Zeke's breath caught. "Jake..."

"No worries, little brother. I'm cool."

Yeah, right. Cool like a tempered blade of steel.

"He'll be fine," Garrett murmured from his other side.

Zeke turned his head and encountered an identical steeliness in Garrett's eyes. Come to think of it, the Brotherhood had fallen completely silent. The joking had stopped and every man faced forward in readiness.

The lineup for the arrival of the field trip bus had been nothing like this. Easy camaraderie had dominated that moment.

This was a show of force.

"Here they come!" Claire broke ranks, hurried to the edge of the marked space and hopped up and down. Taking off her Stetson, she waved it back and forth as she called out to her grandparents.

Zeke closed the gap separating him from Jake and the right side of the line shifted to maintain unity.

His parents were an attractive couple, both fit and well-dressed. He used to be proud of that. Now, seeing them together with their matching leather carry-ons, his stomach pitched.

They were a lie perpetrated by the silver-haired man he now called Bud. His mother, still blonde thanks to a talented hairdresser, and youthful because of good genes and an exercise routine, was a victim.

She waved back to Claire and blew her kisses. Bud focused on the Brotherhood and a muscle worked in his jaw.

"He's intimidated," Jake said in a low voice. "Excellent."

"Does he look any different to you?"

"Other than the white hair? Nope. Eleven years have barely touched the guy. Does he still put cream on his face every night?"

"Yessir."

"Vain bastard."

"Guess it works."

"Or he's made a deal with the devil. I prefer that theory." Jake sucked in a breath and blew it out. "Your mom looks nice."

"She is nice." His throat tightened as she ran to Claire, crouched down and scooped her into a hug.

"Rips your heart out."

"Yes, it does." He cleared his throat. "I'd better go meet her."

He walked toward his mother as Claire wiggled out of her grasp and raced to hug her grandfather. His mom stood and gazed at him, her smile wobbly.

"Hey, Mom." He wrapped her in his arms and breathed in the perfume that had meant *mom* all his life. "Missed you."

She swallowed. "Missed you, too. I know about Jake."

He went still. "You do?"

"Your father told me a week ago, before we made the reservations."

He drew back and searched her face. She had tears in her eyes, but her expression was resolute and surprisingly calm. "Are you okay?"

"I've always suspected he had a secret from his past. Something big he was keeping from me. It's almost a relief to know what it was."

A secret from his past. She had less than half the story. He'd tread carefully. "I'm glad he told you, but Claire thinks you don't know."

She glanced over her shoulder. Behind her, Bud had crouched so he was eye-level with Claire. Clearly they were having a heart-to-heart, with Claire nodding as he talked. "He's telling her, now."

"Well, then. That'll make things easier on her."

"And you. And Jake for that matter."

"I suppose."

"He realized the position he was putting you in."

"He did?"

"Oh, yeah. It was a come-to-Jesus moment for your father."

"Hm." He doubted Bud had ever had such a moment or ever would.

"I was desperate to see you guys and it looked like you wouldn't be coming to us. I even said I'd come by myself if he couldn't make it. That's when he told me."

"I see."

"He didn't want to make you and Claire responsible for keeping this big secret from me."

Zeke wasn't about to give Bud that much credit. More likely he was afraid his wife would follow through on her threat to come alone and stumble upon the secret while she was here. He had to cover his ass before it was handed to him.

"Hello, son." Bud had an adoring Claire tucked in close.

Couldn't very well punch a guy who was holding a hostage. Not that Zeke would do that. Much as he'd love to. "Hey, Bud." He gave him a quick, one-armed hug.

Bud's silver eyebrows arched, but he didn't comment on the use of his first name. "Guess we need to go meet this Brotherhood we've been hearing so much about."

Zeke bristled. "The *Brotherhood* happens to be a—"

"Yeah!" Claire gave a little hop. "My uncles! Come on, Gramma and Grampa! They got all dressed up to meet you. Don't they look awesome?"

His mom's approving gaze swept over them. "They're an impressive bunch, all right."

"True, true." Bud's chuckle revealed a touch of nervousness. "Wouldn't want to get on the bad side of those guys."

Zeke allowed himself a grim smile. *Too late, Bud.*

28

Nell had invited Val back to her place to finish their lunch. The iced tea wasn't cutting it and they'd just uncorked a bottle of wine when her phone played *Head Over Boots*.

"Who's that?" Val pulled two wine glasses from the cupboard.

"Zeke." She glanced at the time. "He can't possibly be home from Great Falls yet." She picked up. "Hey, there."

"Hi. Listen, we're all headed back to the ranch and we just asked the folks if they're up for a barbeque at Henri's tonight. They are, so it's on. You're invited and so's Val. Teague and Ed will be there. They've offered to swing by and give you two a ride."

"Uh, okay. Just a sec. Val's right here. Let me check with her." She put the phone on mute. "We're both invited to a welcome barbeque for Zeke's parents at Henri's tonight. Teague and Ed will be coming and they've offered to give us a ride out to the ranch."

Val's eyes widened. "What the—"

"I can tell Zeke we've planned to see a movie tonight. We don't have to go."

"*We* don't have to, but you should. These people could end up being your in-laws."

"I doubt that. Zeke's made it very clear we're not on that trajectory."

"Then Zeke's not paying attention. You guys are in L.O.V.E. The happily-ever-after kind. Anybody can see that."

Hello pot, meet kettle. "I'm not going if you're not. Friends don't leave friends who've just had a bad breakup."

"Well, I don't want you to stay home because of me. Besides, you know Claire wants us to meet her grandparents."

"We could set up an alternate time."

"Yeah, but this party is Claire's big ta-da moment. We can't have Zeke tell her we'd rather go to a movie."

"Which leaves us with the ride offer. We can drive ourselves. That would help, right?"

"Yes, but the offer makes me think he hasn't told his boss that we broke up. And I really, *really* like Ed. We get along like grits and gravy. I want to keep that relationship. Refusing the ride would be off-putting." She took a deep breath. "We have to ride with them."

"Okay." She unmuted the phone and put it to her ear. "You still there?"

"I am. Thought you might've hung up on me."

"No, I... it's complicated. But yes, we'd both like to come and we'd appreciate a ride from Ed and Teague. Should we let them know or will you—"

"They told me to call if you weren't coming for some reason. Since you are, nothing needs to be done. If you'd be willing to go over to Val's, they'll be at her house at five and they won't have to make two stops."

"I can do that."

"See you soon."

"Can't wait."

"Me, either." He disconnected.

She put the phone on the kitchen counter. "They'll pick us up from your house at five. What do you want to do between now and then?"

Val pushed the cork back in the bottle. "Go grab your party duds and I'll drive you to my place. We can spend a bunch of time on our hair and nails. I've been dying to try doing something special with that curly mop of yours."

"All right, I'm game." At least Val was acting like her old self again. Quite likely because she was about to interact with the man she claimed to hate. "But that won't use up the time."

"I know, but we... wait a minute. We're not driving, are we? We have a lovely designated driver. I meant to say a *ratfink* designated driver. Anyway, while we're getting ready, we can sip wine. That'll drag out the process."

"A *little* wine. I'm not arriving tipsy."

"Me, either. But considering the circumstances, I'm not arriving sober, either."

* * *

The drive to the Buckskin with Teague and Ed was surreal for Nell, especially because she had a slight buzz from the wine. Somehow she and Val had finished a bottle and their snacks hadn't been robust enough to soak up the alcohol. Teague drove and Ed insisted Val had to sit in front. Ed and Nell took the roomy back seat.

The temperature in the front seat was several degrees below zero, but after two minutes, Nell forgot about the quarreling lovers. She was thoroughly entertained by Edna Jean Vidal, championship barrel racer. The woman was just plain fun—curious about Nell's world and willing to share juicy tidbits about her own.

"We had the *best* time today," she announced. "The Brotherhood should go gallivanting around more often so we can do more Buckskin Ranch takeovers."

"They wouldn't let me help, either." Teague broke his self-imposed silence. "They said it was a women-only day."

Val muttered something under her breath and glanced out the window.

"More specifically—" Ed looked over at Nell. "It was women-of-a-certain-age day. Except for Lucy, our token young'n. She's our proof we're not ageist."

"So anybody can be a Babe?"

"Yes, but first we have to like them. Then they must be barrel-racers and either own, borrow or rent a buckskin. You interested? You've already passed the first test."

"That's great to know, but the other two requirements are beyond me for now."

"I'm an excellent teacher, even better than my younger self."

"I believe that."

"I like being eighty-six. I used to lie about how old I am, but I quit doing that."

"You could certainly get away with it," Nell said. "You don't look your age."

"I know, but I went the other way. I told people I was a hundred and two."

"Oh!" She grinned. "That must have been interesting."

"It was. They'd fall all over themselves saying how amazing I looked for a hundred and two. But recently, folks have been nodding in agreement as if they believe me. Do I look a hundred and two?"

"No, ma'am."

"Right answer. By the way, Val was saying a nine-year-old proposed to her. Has that happened to you?"

"Not yet."

"Well, if it does, here's my advice. Stay in touch with that youngster. Eventually it could work out. Younger men make terrific lovers."

"I'll keep that in mind."

Leaning closer, Ed lowered her voice. "I sense a disturbance in the Force."

Nell clapped a hand over her mouth to stifle a giggle. She should have stopped with one glass of wine.

"Don't look so surprised," Ed murmured. "I know all about *Star Wars*. I have connections in Tinsel Town." She ducked a little lower, jabbed a thumb toward the front of the truck and mouthed the word *issues* while raising her eyebrows.

Nell ducked down, too, put her hand up to shield her mouth and murmured *I'm not at liberty to say.*

"Cut it out, you guys," Val said. "I know you're talking about us."

Ed straightened. "Then here's my question. Are you two on the outs?"

"No," Teague said. "We've had a temporary misunderstanding." He looked over at Val. "But we'll work it out."

Val gave him a sunny smile. "In due time."

"I hope so." Ed sighed. "You're the first one he's brought home I've liked." Then she abandoned the subject and asked Nell what she thought about phonics.

That topic took up the rest of the drive while Teague and Val sat in silence, occasionally sending each other intense stares. Passion and fury looked similar, so Nell gave up trying to interpret what was going on.

Henri's party continued the weird vibe. Claire was thrilled to see them and immediately dragged her grandparents over. Nell instantly liked Zeke's mom and wanted to slap his genial, very good-looking dad.

When Zeke showed up, Val engaged Frannie and Bud in an animated discussion of line dancing, allowing Nell and Zeke to edge away from the group.

He took her arm and steered her over to a quiet corner of the yard. Stress showed in every line of his body. He kept his voice down. "Bud told my mom about Jake."

"Bud?"

"My dad. I'd rather call him Bud."

"He told her *tonight*?"

"No, last week, before they booked the cabin. She'd threatened to come alone if he couldn't make it, so I think he got scared. If she came alone, she might uncover his entire scheme."

Nell glanced around to make sure no one was listening. "Then she still doesn't know he's also married to Jake's—"

"I'm sure he didn't reveal that." He drew her further away from the crowd. "If he had, the wheels would have come off the bus. Mom's adjusting to the reality of Jake, but I'm positive she thinks Jake's mother was out of the picture when they got married."

"Oh, Zeke. It's like a soap opera."

"Don't I know it. Mom's still in Bud's corner. Jake and I are ready to wring his neck. Meanwhile Claire..." He sighed. "I guess that's the good news. Claire's oblivious. She's super excited to introduce all her new friends to her grandparents and that's blinding her to any tension going on."

Nell placed a hand on his chest. "Like yours? You're tight as a drum."

"I am." He covered her hand with his. "But there's another piece of good news. Mom's asked Claire to stay overnight in their cabin while they're here."

"The whole time?"

"Yes, ma'am."

"I hardly know what to say."

He gave her a soft smile. "Think you'll get tired of me?"

"No way."

"Then I'll drive you home tonight."

"Awesome."

"Gotta go. I'll find you when the evening winds down."

"Please do." He rejoined his parents and she looked for Val and Teague. They'd migrated to opposite sides of the yard. Claire had brought CJ, Isabel and Cleo Marie into the limelight. Zeke's mom lit up when she saw the baby, but his dad looked bored. What a piece of work.

"So, Nell, we meet at last."

She turned in the direction of the voice and her gaze collided with warm blue eyes.

The woman was tall, with short gray hair in a stylish cut. "I'm Henri." She held out her hand. "Claire's been raving about you for months. I'm so glad you were able to come tonight."

"I am, too. Thanks for inviting me."

"Of course!" Henri lifted her champagne flute. "Can I get you one?"

"No, thanks." She smiled. "I need to keep my wits about me tonight."

"I understand."

"And before I forget, thank you for allowing Zeke to use Prince for the riding lessons. Tatum, the girl riding him, loves him to death. She's determined to become a barrel racer and have her own buckskin someday."

"So I heard. I've tried to get there for one of the lessons, but something always comes up. Maybe next Monday."

"At least the Lassiters will be gone."

Henri looked their way. "Which will be a relief. What do you think?"

"She seems nice. Because of what I know, I couldn't like him if I tried."

"Same here. Poor Zeke. Jake, too. What a miserable situation for them." She turned back to Nell. "I'm glad you and Zeke have become so close, though. I'm sure that helps him cope."

"I like to think so."

"You probably haven't had time to think about my offer, but I—"

"Your offer?"

She blinked. "Zeke didn't mention it? We talked yesterday, and I knew he was going over to your place after the meeting last night, so I thought by now... well, he's had a lot on his mind."

"That's for sure. What was it?"

"Just a suggestion. I could rent one of the guest cabins to you at whatever rate you're paying in town. The obvious disadvantage is the distance from your school."

Her stomach bottomed out. "That's very... generous." Why hadn't Zeke told her?

"Zeke said you loved being within walking distance from school, so you'll probably want to think about it. Clearly it would allow you and Zeke to spend more time together. Claire would be over the moon."

"Have you said anything to her?"

"Oh, no. That's not my place. But she's one of the reasons I'm offering. She adores you. And I adore Claire. She's so excited that you and Zeke are seeing each other."

"I can tell." Nell struggled to breathe normally. "She's such a romantic."

"Yes, she is. Anyway, no pressure on this. The offer's good indefinitely. Take your time deciding. Zeke seemed worried about that long commute, so—"

"That wouldn't bother me."

"No? That's encouraging. Just let me know. Oh, and it would be a two-bedroom, in case..." She smiled. "I guess I'm a romantic, too."

Someone called out for Henri and she turned. "I'd better go check on Ben. He's manning the grill. We can talk more later."

"You bet. And thank you." Henri and Claire weren't the only romantics around here. She hadn't wanted to admit that she'd started dreaming of the fairytale ending, too.

But Zeke hadn't relayed Henri's offer last night. She could understand forgetting to play the ringtone. She'd forgotten about it, too.

This, though, could be life-changing. He wasn't likely to have forgotten it. If anything, their passionate lovemaking should have kept it top of mind. Would he ever have told her? She'd just have to ask him.

29

Although Claire protested mightily that she should get to stay up past her bedtime, the odds were against her, and Zeke was glad for that. She needed sleep.

Her grandparents were in favor of getting her tucked in by her usual bedtime of nine. CJ and Isabel were ready to take Cleo Marie home and they'd offered to run the folks back to their cabin on the way.

Claire came over to Zeke for one last try. "Daddy, if you said I could stay up, I'll bet they'd let me. With all these people, we could catch a ride later. Grampa Bud's waffling. Gramma Frannie's the one you need to talk to."

He crouched down so they were eyeball-to-eyeball. "Are you suggesting I veto my mother's wise decision?"

"Um, not *veto*, exactly. Just try to talk her out of it."

He smiled. "That didn't work when I was your age and it wouldn't work now. She's as firm about bedtime as I am."

"So *that's* where you get it."

"Yes, ma'am."

She heaved a mighty sigh. "Then I'd better start hugging people."

"You can begin with me."

"Okay, Daddy." Sliding her hands under his armpits, she reached as far as she could and squeezed him tight. "I love you."

She said it all the time, but tonight it made him misty-eyed. His lack of sleep must be getting to him. When he hugged her, she felt taller, likely because she was. She'd grown an inch since they'd moved here, one of the reasons she had on a new pair of jeans. "I love you, too, sweetie."

Letting go, she backed away, mischief in her eyes. "I have a lot of people to hug. That'll take a long time, y'know."

"Claire. People are waiting."

"Okay, okay. I'll make it snappy. Are you coming to get me at sunup?"

"I sure am, pardner."

She grinned. "See ya then, pardner." She hurried off to make her rounds.

After she finished her routine and left with his folks, Jake wandered over, a bottle of cider in each hand. He offered one and Zeke took it. "How're you doing, little brother?"

"About like you, I expect." He lifted the bottle. "Thanks. I've been going easy on this stuff tonight."

"Me, too. But since they're leaving, I wanted to toast their departure." Jake stared in the direction of the parking lot as CJ's truck rumbled to life. "Bud thinks he's taken care of things. That this fixes it."

"But not for either of our moms."

"Nope." Jake took a sip from his cider bottle. "It's time to hold his feet to the fire."

"Can we keep Claire out of it?"

Jake nodded. "I feel a Brotherhood meeting coming on. Tomorrow night would be good. Let's say nine-thirty, around the fire pit. Your mom will have put Claire to bed by then. We invite your dad to the meeting as our special guest. I'll pick him up."

Zeke stared at him. "You're not literally going to put his feet to the—"

"No, no." His eyes glittered. "It's a tempting fantasy, but I couldn't do it. Even more important, Charley would never resort to something like that. He was the least violent man I've ever known."

"So what's the plan?"

"Not sure, yet. I need to talk it over with Matt and see if he's on board for a meeting. If it's a go, I'll run my ideas by you if there's any way we can talk in private. If not, just follow my lead at the meeting."

"I'll do my best to answer if you contact me tomorrow. Most of the day I'll be with Claire and my folks."

"Figured that." His gaze was steady. "And I realize that having Claire stay with your mom gives you a chance to head out to Nell's tomorrow night, but—"

"I'll be at the meeting. Wouldn't miss it."

"Good." The light of battle had returned to his eyes. "This isn't over."

* * *

Zeke got a kick out of watching Nell and Val interact with the Babes. Something Josette said had them both doubled over with laughter. Then Pam executed a hip-swinging dance move, circling in place with her hand in the air. She pointed to Nell, who copied the maneuver perfectly. Val followed suit. Soon they were all doing it to whatever music was in their heads.

"I'm crazy about that woman, Zeke."

He turned. Teague stood a few feet away, his attention focused on Val.

"Word has it that she's into you, too."

"Old news, buddy." He came closer and lowered his voice. "We flamed out."

"Seriously?"

Teague nodded, his jaw tight. "According to her, we're finished."

"What happened?"

"Premature proposal."

"Really?" Zeke's jaw dropped. "You asked her after a week? What's wrong with you?"

He shrugged. "She's the one. I knew it the day we met. But she says that's impossible."

"I happen to agree with her. That's not a rational move, my friend. Tell me you're not on something."

"I'm high on her, is all. I thought it was mutual. I just knew she'd say yes. Instead she broke up with me."

"Think you two can come back from that?"

"Don't know. Time will tell."

"I wish you luck."

"Thanks. I'll need it. I'm guessing Nell won't be riding home with us tonight?"

"No. I'm taking her home." The words brought a rush of heat. "Think I'll go see if she's ready to leave."

"I'm happy for you, Zeke."

"I appreciate that." He gave Teague's shoulder a squeeze. "Maybe you can smooth it over."

"We'll see." He glanced at the group of women. "At least she still likes Ed."

"It's a start." Pouring the rest of his cider into the grass, he put the bottle in a recycling bin before heading toward Nell.

She spotted him coming and said something to the others before walking in his direction. "Is it time?"

"Up to you. I don't want to pull you away if—"

"We can go. I'll grab my purse." She made a detour and fetched if from the pile on one of Henri's garden benches.

Was she tired? That could explain the lack of enthusiasm in her voice. Except a few minutes ago she'd been laughing and dancing around with the Babes.

"Is anything wrong?" He took her hand as they walked to his truck.

"I have something I need to ask you about, but it can wait until we get going."

"Okay." The way she said that set off alarm bells. "Does it have to do with Val and Teague? He told me there was a problem." *Please let it be about Val and Teague.*

"There is a problem, but that isn't what I want to talk about."

Hey, it could be anything. Maybe she'd like to discuss his folks now that she'd met them. She'd want to keep that conversation private. Yeah, it was probably about his folks.

He could tell her that Jake was working on an intervention. The Brotherhood meeting would cut down on how much time they'd have tomorrow night, but she'd be fine sacrificing a couple of hours to such an important cause.

Anyway, they'd have Sunday night, more than they'd ever been allowed. Maybe they'd cook dinner together. Or he could take her to the Moose, just the two of them.

When they reached the passenger side of his truck, he paused. "Before we get in, look up."

She tilted her head back. "Wow. You weren't kidding. I can see twice as many out here. Maybe three times as many. What an awe-inspiring view."

"I'm glad I remembered. Sometimes I take the stars for granted, but I try not to." He opened the door and helped her in. "I think I know what you want to talk about."

"You do?"

"My folks, mostly my dad. Don't worry. Jake has a plan. I'll tell you about it on the way back to town." He shut the door, rounded the front of the truck and climbed behind the wheel. "Jake's checking with Matt to see if we can have a Brotherhood meeting around the fire pit tomorrow night about nine-thirty. And invite Bud. Claire should already be asleep when Jake picks him up at the cottage." He started the truck, backed out of his spot and headed down the sloping driveway.

"Sounds interesting."

"Oh, it will be. I have to be there, so I'll be late coming over to see you, but I figure you won't mind, under the circumstances."

"Not a problem."

"If you were worried about whether he'll continue to get away with victimizing both our moms, he won't. We'll find a way to set things right. And we'll keep Claire out of it. That's important."

"Definitely." She drew in a breath. "But that isn't what I want to discuss."

"All right." He glanced over at her. She was staring straight ahead, her hands clenched in her lap. Anxiety gripped him, stealing his breath. "What, then?"

"Henri mentioned something tonight and it got me to thinking about our situation."

He tightened his hold on the wheel. "What did she say?"

She looked at him. "Why didn't you tell me she'd be willing to rent me one of the Buckskin cabins?"

He swallowed. "Because you love being close to the school."

"I would love being close to you and Claire, too."

"I see." Cold sweat trickled down his spine. "You'd have a long commute five days a week. Don't you think you'd get sick of that?"

"Not if it means I'd get to live on the ranch, which is beautiful, and look at the stars every night. And be with you and Claire more often." An undercurrent of tension colored her words.

He heaved a sigh. "I didn't tell you—or Claire—about Henri's offer because I'm not willing to risk what Claire and I have for something that might not work out. If it didn't, there would be no going back. That failure would seep into the fabric of our lives at the Buckskin. Things would never be the same."

"Nothing ever stays the same, Zeke."

"You're right. But for now, when it comes to Claire and me, things are at least stable. I want to maintain that."

"I thought I could, too. Until now. I was grateful for the time we had. There were no good alternatives, so I accepted the limitations." Tension had become anger. Her voice vibrated with it. "But Henri's invited me to come and stay, which means we could see each other more—"

"Only if Claire and I move into the guest cabin with you."

"Not true. We could have meals together, go riding together, hang out at the barn together."

"But ultimately you'd want Claire to give up her bunkhouse."

"Is that such a big deal?"

His jaw tightened. "You know it is. You saw how proud she was to show it—"

"But she's campaigning to get us together! Do you really think the bunkhouse matters?"

"Yes, damn it. She hasn't connected the dots."

"Then connect them for her! See what she says."

"I'm not doing that. She's only eight. She has some movie version of what it would be like if you were part of our lives. She has no idea what kind of issues we—"

"What issues?"

"I don't know, but there are always issues."

"Of course! And you work through them."

"Or they tear you apart and everything's ruined!"

"You can't know that in advance. If you…" She gulped. "If you care about someone—"

"You look before you leap."

"Or you take a leap of faith."

He dragged in a breath that hurt going in and even more going out. "Nell, you're asking more than I'm ready to give."

She was silent for several seconds. "And you're asking more than I'm willing to give."

The pain slicing through his chest made him gasp. He covered it with a cough. "So that's it?"

"I think it is, Zeke."

He gripped the wheel to keep his hands from shaking. "What do you want to do?"

"Drop me at Val's."

"Then what? Do we continue the riding lessons with the girls?"

"Oh, crap."

"Don't pull out of that." If it sounded like he was begging, he was. "Please."

"I wouldn't. I can't. It's not fair to them."

A life raft. A flimsy one, but something to hold on to. "Look, this is Claire's special weekend. What if we keep this discussion between us? Nobody has to know, yet, especially her."

"I can do that. Except for Val. I'll be talking to her. But she'll keep quiet."

"You'll have to direct me to her house. I've never been there."

She gave him directions. When he pulled up, Val and Teague were on the porch having a heated discussion involving lots of arm waving. Ed was sitting sideways in the back seat with the door open so the dome light was on. She was eating something as she watched the drama on the porch.

Zeke cruised by and glanced at her. "Still want me to drop you here?"

"Why not? I'll go sit in Ed's truck and talk to her until it's over. It's not like this night could get any worse."

"That's for damned sure."

30

Although Zeke insisted on helping her out of his truck, Nell made short work of the maneuver and headed straight toward Ed's ringside seat. Ed's brand of humor was exactly what she needed. She didn't look back as Zeke drove away.

Ed had a small cooler next to her and whatever she was eating had left dark crumbs on her jeans. She looked up as Nell approached. "Coming to join me?"

"If you don't mind."

"Pardon my nosy question, but why are you here? I had the impression you and Zeke were going back to your house for some hoochie-coochie."

"Changed my mind."

"Ah. Then I'm glad to have the company. Take the front seat if you want a clear view. I'm keeping an eye on the proceedings. I have a vested interest."

"Me, too." Nell opened the front passenger door and sat sideways, like Ed.

"Want a mini chocolate cupcake?"

"Sure." She took the cupcake Ed handed over the headrest. "Thanks."

"Take two. They're small."

"Okay." She accepted a second one. "Can you tell what's happening?"

"I could if they'd start yelling, but they're keeping it down, darn it. This is more like watching a silent movie with no subtitles."

"Judging from their body language, Teague is trying to make his case and Val's having none of it."

"He shouldn't have proposed so quick. I wish he'd talked to me about it first. Now his junk's in the wringer."

"He definitely screwed up. She told him from the beginning she didn't want to make a commitment."

"Men never believe that."

"Some women don't, either." She devoured a cupcake in two bites. "These are great."

"My chef is a genius. So you and Zeke are breaking up, too?"

"I'm not at liberty to say." She popped the entire second cupcake into her mouth.

"Which means you're splitsville. I'm sorry, honey."

The cupcake practically melted in her mouth, almost no chewing necessary. "Me, too. Do you have more cupcakes?"

"Here. Take the cooler up there with you. Finish 'em off."

"Thanks." She hauled the cooler into her lap and counted ten of the little chocolate miracles. "Are you sure?"

"Help yourself. I don't need any more."

"Maybe I'll save some for Val."

"By all means. Hey, since Zeke's history, can I interest you in Teague? From the looks of things, he's striking out with Val and I like you a lot, too."

She finished off another cupcake. "I'm flattered, but I—"

"You're right. Never mind. Val's your best friend. Bad idea. It's a shame about you and Zeke, though."

"FYI, we agreed to keep quiet about it. We don't want to spoil Claire's special weekend."

"Don't worry about me. I'm a vault. I have a secret about Jimmy that I'll take to the grave."

"Jimmy who?"

"Stewart."

"You knew him?"

"Played cards with him on the set of *The Man Who Shot Liberty Valance.* We—uh-oh, show's over. Here comes Teague. He doesn't look happy, poor guy."

"Nope." She winced as Val slammed the door.

"I'll take your seat up front, if you don't mind."

"You bet. I'll go check on Val."

"Take the cooler with you."

"Thanks, I will. Hey, Teague."

He paused. "Nell? What are you doing here?"

"I need to talk to Val."

"But... where's Zeke? Oh, no. You guys broke up. That's the only reason you'd be—"

"Don't say anything. We want to keep it quiet. For Claire's sake."

"Yeah, okay. Sorry, Nell." He glanced at Ed. "Ready to go?"

"I am. Oh, wait a sec. Be a dear boy and fetch a bottle of champagne from the ice chest in the truck bed, please. Nell and Val need something to wash down the cupcakes."

"Yes, ma'am." He headed toward the tailgate.

"Ed, you don't need to give us that. It's expensive stuff."

"Honey, passing out bottles of champagne is what I do." She lowered her voice. "Check with Val," she murmured. "She might give you the green light." She tilted her head in Teague's direction. "Rebound sex can be fun."

"Thanks for the tip, but I don't think—"

"Don't knock it 'til you've tried it." She turned as Teague approached with the champagne. "I was just saying to Nell that you two—"

"Thanks so much for the champagne." Nell snatched the bottle from him and backed up the walkway toward the porch. "Have a nice... drive home."

"Misery loves company!" Ed called over her shoulder as Teague helped her into the truck.

Nell waved as they drove away. Then she turned and started up the steps.

Val flung open the door. "So help me, Teague Sullivan—" She paused in mid-step, her mouth open. "Nell?"

"In the flesh."

"Why aren't you with Zeke?"

"Because—"

"His dad? Claire?"

"We broke up."

"*No.* Damn it, Nell. I hate hearing that."

"I hate saying it, but it's true."

Val sighed. "Come on in." She stepped back. Then she blinked as Nell walked through the door. "Is that a bottle of Ed's champagne?"

"Yep. She just gave it to me before they left."

"When I heard the truck leave and footsteps, I thought Teague had talked her into going home and leaving him here." She closed the door.

"Nope, just me." She held up the cooler. "I also have eight of those mini chocolate cupcakes."

"Ed's the best. Come on in the kitchen. We'll uncork that bad boy and drown our sorrows while you tell me what happened." Opening a cupboard, she took down a couple of wine glasses. "I don't have flutes, so these will have to do."

"I'd drink this out of a water glass." Nell put the bottle and the cooler on the kitchen table and started peeling off the foil. "Are you good at opening champagne? I hardly ever buy it and the few times I have I've made a mess."

"Me, too. But who cares? Everything's a mess tonight."

Nell started unscrewing the cork. "Then you'd better put the glasses on the table so I can start pouring if it—oh, God, there it goes!" As champagne erupted from the neck of the bottle, she splashed as much as she could into the wine glasses.

She set the dripping bottle on the table away from the puddle of champagne surrounding the glasses. "Don't ever tell Ed I wasted some of her expensive champagne."

"Who says it's wasted?" Holding back her hair, Val leaned down and began slurping up the champagne.

Nell joined her. "We're never telling anybody about this, either."

"Like Ed says, I'm a vault."

"Did you know she played cards with Jimmy Stewart?"

"Did you know she had a fling with Clint Eastwood? I wanna be Ed when I grow up."

"I'll bet Ed never licked champagne off the kitchen table."

"I'll bet she's licked it off some hot guy's six-pack, though." Val straightened. "That's most of it. I'll get a dishcloth to get the rest and wipe off the glasses."

When she finished, she picked up one and handed the other to Nell.

Nell gazed at her. "What shall we drink to?"

"To Ed, the founder of the feast."

"To Ed." Nell clicked her glass against Val's and sipped. "It tastes better in a glass."

"I dunno. The taste of dissolving varnish gave it a little extra zip."

"Varnish?"

"I'm teasing. It wasn't on there long enough to dissolve very much." She pulled out one of the kitchen chairs. "Let's break out those cupcakes while you tell me what happened."

After Nell relayed the info about Henri's offer and Zeke's dismissal of it, Val sighed. "It's ironic. You want a commitment from your guy and

I'm running as fast as I can to avoid one with... well, he's not *my* guy."

"Ed suggested I check with you first, and if you're okay with it, I should have rebound sex with Teague."

Val's gaze met hers. "Would you do that?"

"Of course not! And he is so *your guy.* You should see your face. What are you going to do if he starts dating someone?"

"He said tonight he has no interest in going out with anyone else."

"Do you believe him?"

"I don't want to, but he gets this intense look in his eyes when he says it."

"He's planning to wait you out."

"Then he'll have a long damn wait." She poured them each more champagne. "How about you? What if Zeke takes up with some sweetie-pie?"

"I doubt he will." But the possibility made her insides twist. "I'm the first since his divorce, and Claire pushed him into dating me. She's a loyal little kid. I doubt she'd like it if he dated someone else."

"Claire. I forgot about how this will affect her."

"I'm not going to let on that we broke up and Zeke said he wouldn't, either."

"Right, because Claire's so dense. She'll *never* pick up on the fact that you're acting weird with each other." Val rolled her eyes. "Airtight plan, girlfriend."

"What am I supposed to do? He acts like he's madly in love with me, but he won't consider taking the next step."

"You could keep having once-a-week sex with him, I suppose."

"That's no longer an option. Not when he has no faith in me. Not if he doesn't believe in us."

"Nell, he can't." Val reached over and squeezed her arm. "He doesn't even believe in himself."

31

    Zeke could count on one hand the nights he'd spent alone in the past nine years. This was by far the loneliest. He wanted to blame Henri for the debacle but that didn't wash.

    All fingers pointed to him. If he'd broached Henri's plan to Nell last night and explained why he didn't want to go forward with it, she *might* have been willing to listen to his side. Maybe not, but that had been his only shot. He'd blown it.

    He slept fitfully and was up long before dawn. Nell had cut him out of her plans, her dreams, her life. She'd left a hole the size of Montana in his heart.

    Could he make that leap of faith she'd asked of him? He picked up his phone a hundred times and always put it down again. If he only had himself to consider, then maybe he'd risk it. But he'd be putting Claire's happiness on the line, too. He didn't have that right.

    When his phone pinged with a text, he grabbed it, heart thumping. Maybe Nell had—nope. Jake.

Text me when you get back from Nell's. I'd like to run by the bunkhouse for a few minutes and fill you in.

Zeke sucked in air until his heart settled down. *I'm here.*

Okay, then. Climb down from Cloud Nine. We have an intervention to plan.

Zeke sent him a thumbs-up emoji.

Jake's timing was good. Just like Nell had to tell Valerie, he had to tell his big brother. Otherwise Jake would unknowingly keep making comments that would dig into him like jabs from a hot poker.

He made a pot of coffee. By the time he'd poured two mugs, Jake came through the front door of the bunkhouse.

"In the kitchen," Zeke called out.

"Figured." Jake walked in. "Smelled the coffee." He took the mug and lifted it. "Thanks for this. Slept in a bit, didn't have time to caffeine up."

"Did the party run late?"

"Yeah. Mostly talking about this deal since we didn't have to watch what we said after Teague, Ed and Valerie took off. Anyway, the plan is—"

"I need to tell you something, first."

"Okay." Jake listened in silence, his expression grave, but not surprised. When Zeke stopped talking, his brother exhaled. "I was afraid of this."

"What do you mean?"

"Henri told us about her conversation with Nell. She's gonna blame herself."

"She shouldn't. She assumed I'd say something to Nell last night. I should have."

"Yep." He glanced away. "Déjà vu all over again."

"I don't—"

"I get where you're coming from, little brother. Your life wasn't like mine, but we both got slimed by a narcissist. And we're so afraid we'll be like him that we deny ourselves what we need."

"That's not my problem. I'd take that risk any day, but I don't have the right to put Claire's happiness in jeopardy."

"You're doing it anyway. What if she needs Nell as much as you do?"

"I can't know that! What I do know is that she's happy now, and if Nell moves here and it all goes south, then—"

"Clare still has you. And all of us. Don't let the bastard win, little brother. I almost did. I almost lost Millie."

"But you didn't have a kid. Trust me, that makes all the difference."

"I'm not saying it would be an easy leap to make. Nothing's for sure. But even though you look like him, you're not a selfish bastard. You're a good dad."

His throat tightened. "Thanks, bro." He glanced at the kitchen clock. "You'd better tell me the plan. It's getting late."

* * *

After Zeke and Claire finished barn chores, they spent the morning showing his folks around the ranch. Jake had already issued his invitation to Bud for a men-only evening around the fire pit, so

Bud was especially interested in that part of the tour.

Zeke's perception had sharpened. What he used to see as confidence now looked like bravado. Bud was nervous. No doubt about it, the Brotherhood intimidated him.

Had he always been this critical of Zeke's mom? Probably, although his current uneasiness might be making it worse.

Even Claire called him on it. When she said *that wasn't very nice, Grampa,* Bud's jaw dropped. Then he promptly announced they were all going into town for lunch, his treat.

It was a familiar pattern—mean behavior followed by a reward. A slap, then a hug. But always on his terms. Zeke had lived it. This was the first time he'd seen it.

Maybe he would have if Claire had ever been on the receiving end. For some reason, she'd been spared.

They spent the afternoon in town, going through the shops. Claire came home with bags full of loot, but Zeke had to smile when she stood firm on not trying on *any* dresses. If he hadn't put a stop to it, she would have a youth saddle, though. He'd taken Jared Logan aside and apologized for nixing the purchase.

She had her pick of saddles in various sizes at the Buckskin and over at Ed's. Someday he'd get her a custom saddle and that would be a proud day for each of them. He didn't want to be robbed of that moment because Bud was going for the glory.

After dinner in the guest dining hall and a few hands of poker in his folks' cabin, he helped his mom put Claire to bed while Bud smoked a cigar out on the porch.

His mom kissed Claire goodnight. "Sleep tight, sweetheart." She glanced at him. "I'm gonna go check on your dad."

She did that a lot. It hadn't made a big impression until today. She hovered around Bud, a trace of anxiety in her expression, as if she was responsible for his happiness. Zeke didn't like it.

Sitting on the edge of the guest room bed, he smiled at Claire. "Have a good day?"

"I love having them here. Grampa's a little bossy, but I can handle him."

Zeke laughed. "Yes, you can." He glanced around the cozy room. "Miss the bunkhouse?"

"I do, but this is nice, too."

"Yeah?" Interesting. "What do you like about it?"

"It's a log cabin. It's got a fireplace instead of a wood stove. I can pretend I'm a pioneer."

"Which one do you like better?"

"Well, the bunkhouse is cool, especially when the Brotherhood comes over. But this place has a nicer bathroom...." She frowned in concentration, then let out a dramatic sigh. "I give up. I can't pick. They're both good."

"Then it's nice you can have both, huh?" Amazing. He would never have guessed she'd say that.

"It's very nice. I'm lucky."

"Me, too." He leaned down, gave her a hug and a kiss, and stood. "Sweet dreams."

"I love you, Daddy."

Daddy again. And not because she wanted something. Maybe she liked feeling like his little girl every so often. And maybe she was way more flexible than he'd given her credit for. More flexible than he was. "Love you, too, sweetie." He turned out the light and left the room a wiser man.

His mom was straightening up the living room, rearranging pillows on the couch and stacking magazines on the end table.

"I take it he's still out on the porch." He couldn't bring himself to use *Bud* when he was talking to her.

"Yes." She stopped fussing with things and came over. "Do you think he's acting strange?"

Yes, because he's scared. "I'm not sure what you mean."

"He's out of his element here, and it makes him nervous. He never approved of your decision to go into this kind of work. It's so different from what he knows."

"And yet it's all I've ever wanted to do."

"Just like Jake. It's eerie how similar you are. And so different from your father."

That was the point, but he didn't say it. "He might not approve of my choice, but he let me know about the Buckskin and Jake. I'll always owe him for that."

"He put himself in a vulnerable spot by telling you. But he did it because he loves you and wants you to be happy."

"I think it was more about Claire." If Bud had one redeeming quality, that was it. He cherished his granddaughter. It could be what saved his neck in the end.

"Maybe. In any case, I don't know what this manly fire pit discussion is all about, but, like I said, your father feels out of his element. Will you keep that in mind?"

"Yes, ma'am." He was counting on it. So was Jake. "See you tomorrow, Mom." He gave her a hug and went out the door past the Adirondack chair and the scent of cigar smoke. "See you at the fire pit, Bud."

"I keep meaning to ask you. Why are you calling me Bud all of a sudden?"

"Seems right, now that I'm an adult."

"You've been an adult for a while, now. You've always called me Dad."

"Guess so." He clattered down the steps. "And now that I'm my own man, I'd rather call you Bud. How's that?"

Bud's snort was filled with ridicule. "Whatever floats your boat."

Another put-down. Par for the course. "See you soon, Bud."

By the time he drove to the bunkhouse and headed out to the fire pit, flames rose from the circle of stones and everyone was gathered except Jake.

"Hey, it's son number two," CJ called out and strummed a few chords of welcome on his guitar.

"You're playing tonight?"

"Yessir. Music soothes the savage beast, y'know. Unless you listen to the words, which in this case are significant. About cheating and such. Think he'll get it?"

"I doubt it. He thinks the rules don't apply to him."

"I'm confused." Rafe handed him a bottle of cider. "Why's Jake bringing him instead of you. Weren't you just over there putting Claire to bed?"

"Jake wanted the honor of escorting him and that seemed fair. He hasn't had the pleasure of Bud's company for as many years as I have."

Rafe nodded. "I used to wish I knew who my dad was. Now that I see what you and Jake have been through, I should probably be thankful."

"Either he didn't stick around long enough to find out he sired you, Rafe," CJ said, "or your mother didn't want him to know you existed. I'm guessing you're better off not knowing."

"Yeah, I'm going with that. Hey, I hear Jake's truck. What song are you starting off with?"

"That Carrie Underwood one, *Before He Cheats.*"

"Good choice," Nick said. "I like what she does to his truck. But isn't it kinda strange coming from you? Doesn't it need a woman for the words to make sense?"

"I'll sing falsetto."

Matt gave a nod of approval. "Do that. We need some comic relief."

"That's the truth," Zeke said. His gut tightened as the rumble of Jake's rig stopped. Truck doors opened and closed. He dragged in a breath.

Then CJ launched into the song in a weird combo of Carrie Underwood's accent and the Bee Gees. Despite his jangling nerves, Zeke grinned.

Leo walked over and stood beside CJ. He began acting out the story, pantomiming slashing tires and bashing headlights with a baseball bat. Bottle in hand, Nick danced a jig while Garrett and Rafe partnered in some sort of disjointed disco move.

When Jake came around the side of the house with Bud, Zeke was laughing so hard he had to lean against one of the Adirondack chairs.

Jake paused at the edge of the circle of light created by the blazing fire and swept an arm to encompass the wonky behavior. "My brothers."

Bud surveyed the scene. "What the hell is this nonsense?"

Zeke's laughter died as he met Jake's gaze. *Your worst nightmare, Bud Lassiter.*

CJ finished the Carrie Underwood song and moved on to Shania Twain's *Whose Bed Have Your Boots Been Under?* Jake fetched Bud a bottle of cider from the tub full of ice and gradually the group settled into the Adirondack chairs. All except Matt, who remained standing, and CJ, who continued his streak with Reba's *Whoever's in New England.*

When CJ finished that number with a flourish and put down his guitar, Matt strolled to a position in front of the fire and faced the semi-circle of chairs. Jake had placed Bud in the middle seat.

Matt focused on Bud. "This meeting of the Buckskin Brotherhood is in session. Bud Lassiter, those tunes were chosen for a reason. Can you guess what that reason is?"

"Haven't a clue." He lounged back in his chair and took a gulp of cider.

"They're a message. But I'll let your two sons spell it out. Jake, you're up."

Jake took Matt's place. "The message is about cheating, Bud. And for you, that activity ends now."

He sat bolt upright. "What the hell?"

"Your two-timing days are over, mister."

"How dare you?"

"How dare *you*? You've had my mother on a roller-coaster of divorce and remarriage. This is the end of the ride. You're going to file for divorce and never see her again."

"You can't dictate to me." Bud pushed out of his chair. "I'll do whatever I damned well—"

"No, you won't." Zeke left his chair and stood beside Jake. "Divorce Jake's mother or we'll reveal everything to my mom."

"You'll ruin their lives!"

"Too late," Jake said. "They're already ruined. They just don't know it. We can turn you in tomorrow and you'll go to jail. But we're offering you a way out. Divorce one woman and keep the other, and we won't file charges."

Bud's face crumpled. "But I love them both."

Jake muttered something that sounded like *bullshit.*

"If you love them both, prove it," Zeke said. "Free Jake's mother from this toxic cycle so she can find someone who will stick with her. And devote the rest of your life to making amends to my mom."

His chin jutted. "I won't do it."

Jake took a step closer, his voice low and menacing. "Then we'll see your ass in jail."

"You wouldn't put your own father in jail."

Zeke moved up beside Jake and looked into eyes so like his. But the man was nothing like him. "You sure about that?"

Bud swallowed. Then he glanced around. The Brotherhood had risen from their chairs, three beside Zeke and three beside Jake.

"Don't test us," Matt said. "You'll lose."

Bud maintained his defiant posture for several long seconds. Then he bowed his head. "Yeah, okay."

"We'll be keeping track," Jake said. "One false step and you're toast."

Bud gave Zeke a furtive glance. "I don't want Claire to find out."

"She won't if you behave yourself. You step out of line and it all falls apart."

He nodded again. "Can I go home, now?"

Zeke looked over at his brother, who gave a curt nod. "Jake and I will take you."

The ride to the cabin was silent. The ride back to the bunkhouse was not.

"Damn, that felt great!" Zeke pounded out a victory beat on the dashboard.

Jake grinned. "Yeah it did. Still does. I'll be cruising on this high for a *very* long time."

"We need to set up a monitoring system. We can't trust him at all."

"I'm aware. We'll keep close track. Millie and I have already planned to make regular visits to my mom. And suggest counseling, if she's open to it."

"Are you going to tell her about my mom and me?"

"I might. She has a hot temper, though. We don't want bloodshed. If she goes along with the counseling idea, then it's more doable." He pulled up to the bunkhouse. The parking lot was empty except for his truck.

"Where'd everybody go?" Zeke unsnapped his seatbelt.

"Home to their ladies. Which is where I'm headed."

"I thought they'd all want to celebrate."

"We will. By making our ladies very happy." Leaving the motor running, he turned in the seat, his gaze steady. "Don't you have somewhere to go, little brother?"

Adrenaline shot through him and he reached for the door handle. "Yes. Yes, I do."

<u>32</u>

After staying awake into the wee hours drinking and commiserating with Val the night before, exhaustion had propelled Nell to bed at nine. Evidently she was overtired, though, because sleep refused to come.

The longer she lay in the dark tossing and turning, the more she wanted to punch something. Damn Zeke Lassiter! She'd found the perfect town, the perfect job, the perfect little bungalow and the perfect best friend. Then that sexy cowboy had to show up and ruin *everything*.

She was a mess—tired, cranky, sexually frustrated. Yep, that, too. What a disaster. How could an intelligent woman get herself into such a fix?

Wait—she was intelligent. And she hadn't taken all those psychology classes for nothing. What techniques were good for letting off steam? Physical exercise, but she wasn't about to go running around the neighborhood at... what was it? Ten-thirty-seven. She'd been trying to sleep since *nine*.

Damn Zeke Lassiter. What else released tension? Well, besides *that.*

Oh, yeah, beating on something soft with a baseball bat. Too bad she didn't have one.

She had a broom, but that would be too long and awkward. Bounding out of bed, she flipped on lights as she roamed the house looking for a bat substitute.

The plastic extension for the vacuum cleaner head was about right, but what if she broke it? She was in the mood to hit something hard and breaking her vacuum attachment would just make her mad at herself. Counterproductive.

She opened her coat closet. Not the umbrella. She'd break that for sure. But the wooden closet rod might work. Thank goodness for old houses that still had wooden rods.

This one was thick and about the same length as a bat. And—hallelujah—it was removable. Unhooking the hangers that held her parka, her raincoat and a denim jacket, she dumped them on the end of the couch.

The rod came out like a dream. She piled two large throw pillows on the other end of the couch, lifted the rod over her head and whacked the top pillow. Yes!

"Take that, Zeke Lassiter!" She pounded the pillow as hard as she could. "And that, and that, and that! You suck! You suck, suck, suck!" Panting, she paused to catch her breath.

What was that noise? She turned toward the door. Someone was tapping on it. Better not be *him*. "Who is it?"

"Me."

Perfect. Her evening was complete. "Go away!"

"Nell, please let me—"

"I'm busy!"

"I know. I heard you whaling away in there."

His voice still had the power to make her stomach flutter. "I'm not having sex with you. Not *ever*. I don't care if the world's coming to an end." She moved closer to the door. "I don't care if you just discovered you have a terminal disease. You can just—"

"I don't want to have sex with you."

"Ha! That's a likely—"

"But I'd sure like to make love to you."

"I knew it! Claire's with her grandparents again tonight and you're lonely."

"Both things are true, but I—"

"You think just because we had such a good time in bed I won't be able to resist your sexy self, but I can and I will. Go *away*." She was close enough to touch the door. And weakening, damn it.

"Please let me in."

She swallowed. "No."

"Then I'll have to say this out here. I was hoping I could say it to your face, but—"

"Say what?" Her heart stuttered.

"I love you."

Oh, and he thought *that* would get him through the door. "Nice try. I already knew that. But you don't have the courage of your convictions."

"I do, now."

She gulped. His tone had changed. He did sound more sure of himself. "What do you mean?"

"I love you and I'm asking you to share a guest cabin at the ranch with me and Claire. I've been an idiot. I hope you can forgive me for that, because—"

She flung open the door, heart hammering. "I'm listening."

He glanced at the rod in her hand. "Would you... uh... mind putting that down?"

"Oh." She tossed it away and it clattered to the floor. "I was using it to get out my frustrations."

"Because I suck."

God, he was adorable, standing there with his Stetson shoved back and his hopeful expression. "You do suck." She paused. "But that's not always a bad thing."

He grinned, relief in his gaze. "You wouldn't make that joke if you were still mad."

"Oh, I'm still mad." She reached for his arm and tugged him inside. "Mad because you put me through hell, mad because it took you so long to figure this out." She gazed up at him. "I'm also mad about you, cowboy."

His breath caught. "Does that mean—"

"That I love you? That I can't wait to move into that guest cabin with you and Claire? Yes, it does."

"Thank God." He kicked the door shut and pulled her into his arms. "Thank God I didn't completely blow it."

All the tight knots in her body loosened. She wrapped her arms around his neck and snuggled in. "You came close."

"Too close." He tightened his grip. "It's scary to think I almost lost you. And by the way, your ringtone is *I Need You.*"

"Oh." She melted against him.

"I need you so much, Nell." He lowered his head.

"Wait."

He paused.

"What changed?"

"Everything." Love shone in the depths of his gaze.

"Like what?"

"Can I explain later? I desperately want to—"

"But I—"

"Just take my word for it. Everything changed." He leaned closer. "Except this." His mouth settled over hers.

As his kiss deepened, as the warm rush of desire mixed with love swept her away, she took his word for it. Everything had changed. Except for this. Which made anything possible.

* * * * *

A premature proposal leaves Teague Sullivan
and Valerie Jenson in a faceoff in
MARRIAGE-MINDED COWBOY, book nine
in the Buckskin Brotherhood series!

* * * * *

New York Times bestselling author Vicki Lewis Thompson's love affair with cowboys started with the Lone Ranger, continued through Maverick, and took a turn south of the border with Zorro. She views cowboys as the Western version of knights in shining armor, rugged men who value honor, honesty and hard work. Fortunately for her, she lives in the Arizona desert, where broad-shouldered, lean-hipped cowboys abound. Blessed with such an abundance of inspiration, she only hopes that she can do them justice.

For more information about this prolific author, visit her website and sign up for her newsletter. She loves connecting with readers.

VickiLewisThompson.com

CPSIA information can be obtained
at www.ICGtesting.com
Printed in the USA
LVHW010947020122
707651LV00004B/832

9 781638 039891